"No One Ever Tames A Great Snowy,"

Charly said with wonder. "Humans have been their enemy for too long, and their instinct to hunt is too strong. Do you want to know about their mating habits?"

Tanner smiled. "Tell me."

"The female Snowy is shy, so when the male comes courting he brings her a gift. The male Snowy will show the lady his courting gift, then hide it under his wing. Then show her. Then hide it again. That's how he gets her to trust him. If she wants the present, she has to come to him." Her eyes glinted with humor. "It's hard to picture our owl acting too romantically. Lord, he's so ornery!"

"Not with his own." Tanner spoke quietly, but Charly could tell that his words were meaningful in more ways than one. "He'd fight anyone or anything to the death who dared to threaten his mate or his young. He's not *supposed* to trust people. He can't." He paused. "You see, Charly, it could mean his life."

Dear Reader:

It takes two to tango, and we've declared 1989 the "Year of the Man" at Silhouette Desire. We're honoring that perfect partner, the magnificent male, the one without whom there would be no romance. From January to December, 1989 will be a twelve-month extravaganza, spotlighting one book each month as a tribute to the Silhouette Desire hero—our *Man-of-the-Month*!

You'll find these men created by your favorite authors utterly irresistible. March, traditionally the month that "comes in like a lion and goes out like a lamb," brings a hero to match in Jennifer Greene's Mr. March, and Naomi Horton's Slater McCall is indeed a *Dangerous Kind of Man*, coming in April.

Don't let these men get away!

Yours,

Isabel Swift
Senior Editor & Editorial Coordinator

JENNIFER GREENE
Night of the Hunter

Silhouette Desire

Published by Silhouette Books New York

America's Publisher of Contemporary Romance

To my readers:

To my knowledge, my hero's career does not exist. I invented it on a whim, a fantasy and a desire to give you a special romantic hero.

SILHOUETTE BOOKS
300 East 42nd St., New York, N.Y. 10017

ISBN: 0-373-05481-5

First Silhouette Books printing March 1989

Printed in the U.S.A.

JENNIFER GREENE

lives on a centennial farm near Lake Michigan with her husband and two children. Before writing full-time, she worked as a personnel manager, counselor and teacher. Mid-1988 marked the publication of her twenty-fifth romance. She claims the critical ingredient to success is a compassionate, kind, patient, understanding husband—who can cook.

Her writing has won national awards from Romance Writers of America, *Romantic Times*, and *Affaire de Coeur*. She has also written under the pen name of Jeanne Grant.

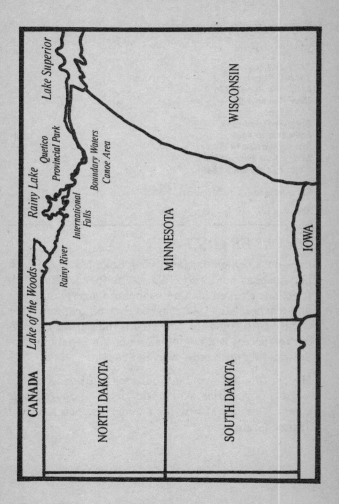

One

Nothing moved. The pale dawn illuminated bare trees, barren fields and a ghost-white blanket of snow. The temperature hovered around zero; the windchill was twenty degrees below that. It hurt to breathe. Hell, it hurt to move. Tanner was punishing cold and punishing tired ... and all for an owl.

The bird skittered ahead another fifteen feet from him, and Tanner mentally swore. The owl knew she was being stalked and had no intention of being captured. Even badly wounded, she managed to maintain a precise distance from him—the exact distance he couldn't make up. Snowshoes inhibited his ability to move quickly; so did the two feet of fresh powder.

What a night. Tanner was used to the exhaustion and cold but not to the dent in his pride. The owl had been battling wits with him for nearly fourteen hours.

She was winning. She couldn't even fly—dried blood had frozen on her damaged wing—but she was still easily getting the best of him. If she wasn't so unbelievably beautiful, he'd say to heck with her.

But she was. Not just beautiful but priceless, precious. Great Snowys were rare now, but as a kid, Tanner had seen a number of the owls in these Minnesota north woods. None had compared with this one.

Except for a few caramel speckles, she was a velvet-pure white. Her head was as round as her body. She appeared neckless and resembled a butterball of a snowman. Such a tiny bit of a thing shouldn't have rated a term like "magnificent," but she was. When open and spread, her wings spanned a full five feet—five feet of that ermine-white regal mantle of feathers, five feet of beauty and power and pride. She was looking at him now. She had huge, fearless, yellow-gold eyes. She was waiting for him. Daring him.

He'd flushed her out of the last sparse stretch of woods and into an open field. She had no cover now. She didn't care. Her barrel chest was heaving from pain, weariness and stress. She blinked at him, slow and lazy and taunting, but he could see the look in her eyes—fierce, wild, proud. She acknowledged no weakness. She intended to die outrunning him.

She was going to die unless he caught her.

In the distance he saw the fenced pasture and the clutch of shadowed buildings—two horse barns and outbuildings surrounding a white frame farmhouse. The property cuddled the Minnesota-Canada border, with the natural boundary of the Rainy River to the north. Tanner had crossed the frozen river twice in pursuit of the owl. Getting lost was no issue. He knew the border country as well as he knew his own heartbeat, and trespassing was no issue. No one ever had to know he was here. The snow drifting down would quickly cover his tracks, and the frigid morning was desolate and dark. There was no reason for a rancher to be up this early, and Tanner needed those buildings.

When he deliberately waved his arms, the owl skittered another few feet away from him, edging closer to the back of the first red-sided horse barn—as he'd hoped. She hadn't worried about that barn yet. Her strength and limited energy reserves were concentrated on her primary enemy—him, as she saw it. For the last mile she hadn't taken her eyes off him. Any minute, though, she was going to catch a whiff of alien "civilized" scents. He was counting on that. When she caught those scents, she'd fluster, make a mistake.

She damn well had to make a mistake soon. Even wearing insulated arctic gloves, his fingers burned like fire. In principle the pain was a comfort—the danger of frostbite began with the loss of sensation—but the pain also warned him he was running a fine edge.

He couldn't go on much longer. The threat of frostbite was only one problem. His lungs ached from breathing in the icy air. His vision was blurring from exhaustion. His legs were going stiff and clumsy on him, his right thigh trying to cramp. His body expected punishment from him, but now that he was thirty-seven, Tanner's muscles refused to be as forgiving as they used to be, and the rifle slung over his shoulder weighed a ton.

Still, as silently and ruthlessly as the predator he was stalking, he moved forward. Closer. Deliberately crowding her, deliberately threatening her with the nearness of his man-scent.

Her talons buried in snow, the owl crept backward, about fifteen feet now from the corner of the horse barn. Her beak was sharp—sharp enough to shred any piece of meat that was too large for her to swallow whole. Still, he wasn't worried about her biting him. Owls didn't use their beaks as weapons. They used their talons, and once prey was within an owl's grasp, the animal rarely escaped. Nature had created the owl's claws with the strength to stab and pierce, the power to kill.

And she just can't wait to use them on you, Tanner. He knew that, just as he knew he was too battered and cold to retrace all those miles, much less toting a big wounded bird. Assuming he caught her, he also had no way of mending her broken wing.

None of that concerned him now. A man familiar with the knife edge of danger rarely wasted time on "hows." When the moment came, he'd find a way to do what he needed to do. He always had. For now, every pulse of blood, every movement he made, every thought in his head focused relentlessly on his only priority. Catching her.

A streak of wind gusted around the corner of the barn. She froze. Tanner couldn't smell the horses yet, but he guessed she had. Horses and owls weren't enemies, but any unfamiliar smell triggered instinctive danger for her now. Her head swiveled back to him, her gold eyes full of rage.

"Stay still, love. Stay still." Although his lips were numb with cold, his voice was like a lover's whisper, tender, soft, sexy. He talked to her, wooing her, as he slipped the rifle's shoulder strap off his arm and propped the gun against the barn. Traveling the north woods without a rifle was foolhardy, but he didn't need it now and the gun inhibited his maneuverability.

The horse scent had thankfully confused her. When he edged closer, she stayed still. He risked another step. "Come on, beauty. Stay put, just for a minute. I don't think you're really that scared of me. You're just hurt, love...."

When he closed in another foot, she valiantly tried to puff up and spread her wings. She wasn't trying to fly—she already knew she couldn't—but her last-ditch defense was to show off her full wing span in a classic threat display. Most predators would be intimidated. All Tanner saw was the dried crusted blood on her one bent wing and the wild look of pain the action caused her.

He whispered to her about what he thought of stupid, stubborn, proud females with pea-size brains. He told her what he thought about her questionable parentage and dubious morals, and he swore at her in three languages—Quebecois French, Spanish and English—all in the sexiest, tenderest, softest croon he could manage.

His croons accomplished precisely nothing, but the woman did. He never actually *saw* her. He simply heard the crunch of boots in snow, saw the pale shadow moving from the far side of the barn and registered that the stranger was female. She didn't matter; his owl did. He guessed this was his chance and it was. The owl turned her head at the new smell, the new threat, and Tanner rushed the last five feet between them.

The bird screeched her rage when he securely wrapped his arms around her wings and lifted her. His grasp couldn't have been more gentle. She wasn't appeased.

Her talons pierced his gloves, drawing blood, and her beak aimed straight for his eyes. She was *not* happy. Neither was Tanner. There was only one way to hold her that wouldn't risk additional injury to her wing, but that hold left him vulnerable. One of her four-clawed talons ripped free and began to shred his down parka. She screamed, snapped, squirmed. For all her huge wing span, she weighed very little—an owl's bones were hollow, her feathers were all weightless fluff. Light or not, she was more than two handfuls to control.

"Just tell me how to help!"

Again he heard the woman more than saw her. Later it would occur to him how calm and soothing her voice was, but not then. Just then all hell was breaking loose in his arms. "Take off your coat." His tone had turned brusque, harsh.

"My coat?"

"Now! Take off your jacket and throw it over her head. Gently. And dammit, fast!"

She did, and thankfully "dammit, fast." The moment the owl's head was covered, the bird went silent—leaving Tanner's heart still pumping adrenaline and his breath still coming in rasps. The total silence was sudden, like a surprise, and gave him his first chance to glance at the woman.

She was no-nonsense tall and rawboned and, without her jacket, was shivering hard. Her arms were clutched around a pink sweater with a fringe of lace at the throat. The sweater accented high rounded breasts, but its lace and color looked totally incongruous paired with a rancher's working denims and calf-high boots. The legs were nice and long but she didn't have much of a fanny. He pegged her age in the late twenties—no lines marred her creamy-white skin but she wasn't spring young, either. Just plain.

Real plain. A thick, dark blond braid swung down her back. Pulled back from her face that way, the hairstyle did nothing to soften the strong bones of her face. Pale eyebrows arched over a dominant forehead. Her chin was a square, her mouth too wide. The composite features had the stamp of character and intelligence—but definitely not beauty, except for her eyes. A man wouldn't forget those eyes too quickly. They were almond shaped and a gold green—like the shine of dark leaves in summer with the sun tipped on them.

The look in her eyes made his own narrow. She was staring at him openly with guileless interest. That wasn't how most women looked at him. At six foot three, with a shag of mink-brown hair speckled white and the build of a lumberjack, he intimidated most strangers—especially women. He wasn't a man of charm and chitchat. If he walked into a bar, most men gave him a wide berth. Once he'd overheard someone say he had a predator's eyes, cold eyes, the eyes of a man looking for trouble. The comment had amused him. It pinned down exactly who he was.

The woman seemed to miss that whole picture. Like a shy fawn who couldn't take her eyes from the wolf, she revealed something in those soft green eyes that made him uneasy—until she focused on the welt on his cheek. "You're bleeding."

Good Lord. Who cared? "I need to use your barn," he snapped, and immediately headed for it. In the best of times, he might have remembered his manners and asked her permission. This was not the best of times. His right thigh was cramped with pain, his hands raw with cold; the razor jabs contributed by his owl stung like a blaze of fire, and something about her sweet low voice grated on him. Hell, anything would have grated on him at this point. He was so tired he could hardly see.

Over his shoulder he called back gruffly, "Go on back in your house before you freeze to death."

"You need a place to put her. My dad used to raise roller pigeons. There's an old empty pigeon coop in a corner of the hayloft—"

"I'll find it." He was still moving.

"But you obviously can't climb to the second story in snowshoes. If you want help—"

"I'll manage."

"How?" The hint of humor came through, even through her chattering teeth. "You can't unlace the snowshoes while you're holding her, and you hardly want to let her go again until she's confined. For heaven's sakes—"

Before he could stop her, she'd whisked in front of him and crouched down. It took her some time to unlace the snowshoes. The leather straps were ice crusted and stiff and her chilled fingers were fumbling. Tanner was comfortable in a blizzard; he took pain for granted and had never backed down from a fight, but the look of the woman kneeling at his feet totally unnerved him.

"I can do it," he said testily.

"What are you arguing for? Of course you can't, not if you hold her at the same time. Just stand still."

He kicked off the left snowshoe when the laces were free, then the right. She'd stood up by then, crossed her arms and buried her cold fingers in her armpits. Again her gaze swept his face. Again he felt...bothered. For a woman built so plain and practical, her interest was unmistakably, shyly feminine. Vulnerable. Maybe that was why he couldn't stop himself from barking at her again. "Thanks, but now get back in your house where you can warm up."

"You're pretty bossy for a stranger." But she obediently started toward her house. He was halfway through her barn door when he heard her call out, "The name's Charly Erickson, by the way."

His mind registered the name, then forgot it and her. The barn was dark inside, filled with the distinctive scents of horses, leather, hay. He didn't bother with a light, just paused so his eyes could adjust to the dimness.

From the look of the dozen filled stalls, she was raising American Belgians—some tawny, some red—but none of the horses that whinnied at his arrival were likely to ever have to pull a plow. He didn't need to see the wall of ribbons and trophies to recognize champion breed. Even a Clydesdale didn't have the muscle and power and style of a prize Belgian.

He noticed that there were three stallions, that four of her mares were pregnant and that two of the horses couldn't be more than yearlings because they hadn't reached their full ton size yet. Mostly he noticed that they'd all been pampered like babies.

Her tack hung from neat hooks, none of it new, all of it the best. He could smell the sweet molasses in the feed. Each stall was big and airy, the pungent hay fresh, the main walkway spotless . . . and Tanner had run out of time for idle curiosity. His pupils had adjusted to the dim light. He glanced at the small partitioned supply room in the far corner. Undoubtedly where she kept her first-aid supplies. But that, too, had to wait.

Climbing the stairs to her hayloft was a clumsy business, partly because his right thigh kept cramping, mostly because of the awkwardness of his jacket-covered cargo. He found the wire pigeon coop at the top of the stairs. The coop was roomy and, beyond a shuttered window and different levels of perches, totally empty. There was no sign of food or bedding, but like everything downstairs, the cage was meticulously clean.

Carefully shifting the bird to free his right hand, Tanner flipped the door latch . . . and decided the woman had a husband. He also decided he didn't like her husband. A man wouldn't have sent a woman to check the sounds of a stranger in their yard at dawn—not a man as Tanner defined one.

While his owl was still blinded, he angled her down to a perch at his chest height. Her talons immediately grasped and held on to the limb. She made a sound. So did he. "Yeah, you're still mad at me, aren't you, love? But let's not pretend to get all riled up because you smell the ghost of a few old pigeons. If you're anything like your breed, you don't care whose house you sleep in. Hell, I don't, either. We're two of a kind, sweetheart."

For a moment he hesitated. He couldn't fix her wing with the jacket covering her, but it was real hard to make himself take it off. She was nice now, docile, still. For her sake as much as his, he wanted to keep her that way.

With one hand he started lifting the weight of the coat off her inch by inch. With the other, he carefully, carefully felt for injuries to her underside that he might not have seen. "Let's negotiate, love. If you're real nice and quiet while I fix your wing, the very minute I'm done—I promise—you can go for my jugular. You'd love that, wouldn't you, beauty? And...hell." When he tossed the woman's jacket in the far corner, he nearly laughed. No longer blindfolded, the owl's eyes fixed him with a rapacious gold stare. "I could be wrong, but I sure didn't notice any equipment to lay eggs, George. So much for the sweet talk. Heck, no wonder you were offended. If I'd known we were dealing man to man, I'd have handled a few things differently."

Below, Tanner heard the whoosh of wind when the barn door opened. He paid no attention. There were just two of them in that coop, two hunters, two predators, two night scavengers and two loners.

Tanner had felt that emotional draw to the Great Snowy from the first, but "George" was in no hurry to recognize the kinship. The owl didn't immediately move to attack, but his posture was stiff and proud and wary. The warning in those fierce gold eyes was unmistakable. *Move an inch closer, human. I dare you....*

Tanner never took his eyes from the bird as he silently stripped off his gloves. The barn had absorbed some creature heat, but it was no oven. He cupped his hands and repeatedly blew into them, needing warmth—any warmth—before he had the flexibility and coordination to help the bird.

Minutes passed before his fingers could move without pain, before his lips stopped feeling like two ice cubes rubbing together. "All right, I'm going to go find you some water, get something for that wing. While I'm gone, I want you to do your best to decide you like me, George. Neither of us is going to have any fun if we have to do this the hard way." When he latched the door, he studied the bird one last time. "Why am I talking? We both know you're going to make this as tough as you possibly can," he said dryly, and headed back down the stairs.

Below, a light had been switched on in the supply room, announcing where the woman was. He searched for her name. Charly. When he paused in the doorway, he saw she'd pulled on a man's old canvas jacket. The hint of pink-and-lace vulnerability had disappeared, and she was moving capably and swiftly around the white-shelved little room. As soon as she noticed him, she started talking in that silky low alto of hers.

"I brought out a thermos of coffee. Maybe you don't like coffee, but I figured you could at least put your hands around a mug and warm them up, and the heater's on.'' She motioned. ''As far as the owl, I don't know what you want. I saw her wing. I have antiseptic and antibiotic I use on the horses, but I don't know if you'd use them for a bird. I can call the vet— Wes Small's semiretired, and he's a great one for fixing wild critters—but the thing is, he's so far, and the roads are closed after last night's snow. It would be a long trek for him by snowmobile—''

He had to do something to stop her monologue. ''It's not a her. It's a George.''

Her head lifted from the tubes and vials she was shuffling through, and her lips tilted in a smile. ''Ah.'' The smile did something to her face, softened the angular lines, muted her plainness. ''No wonder the bird was behaving so badly.''

He might have chuckled at her humor if her soft eyes weren't wandering shyly over him again. She disturbed him. He just couldn't figure her. On the surface, she had the look of the only kind of woman who successfully thrived in this north country: practical, strong, filled with common sense.

But the hint of shyness was out of character for such an obviously capable woman. And the high sweep of color on her cheekbones had nothing to do with the cold. Any thirty-seven-year-old man could recognize sexual vibrations.

Where the hell was her husband? ''Look,'' he said impatiently. ''I don't need a vet, and you don't need to be out here. Go back to your warm kitchen. I'll find whatever I need . . . and pay you for whatever I use.''

''Hmm.'' Her response seemed agreeable, but she continued to sort through bot pastes and powders and sprays until she came up with iodine. "Don't you want the coffee?"

"No."

"Your hands are warm as toast, right? You always this bullheaded, or is it just on Tuesday mornings?"

He didn't doubt that she was only trying to be friendly. Such a simple issue for her, though, was not so simple for him. He said quietly, firmly, "If you're worried I'm going to bother you or anything you have, don't be. You really don't need to be out here."

She didn't seem to hear him. "What are we going to do for a splint? I assume that's what you do for a wing, splint it? I've done more than my share of first aid on dogs' paws and horses' hooves, but birds...." She shook her head. "Why don't you pour a mug of that coffee and just take it easy while you tell me what you want? I know where everything is. You don't. And we'd better get moving here, because you're second on the list of walking wounded. Your hand's a mess. So's your cheek."

"I'm fine," he said impatiently.

"So you keep saying. What's your name, by the way?"

He moved in, checked what she was collecting on the wooden tray and then focused on her shelves. "Tanner. Carson Tanner."

Her hands went still for one swift instant; her eyes darted to him. Although she immediately went back to rummaging for supplies, he guessed she'd recognized his name. Neighbors were few and far between in the border country. When people had the rare chance to get together, they talked.

Nothing she'd heard would make any woman real excited about being with him, even if she was in a crowded room with a man at her side. They were not in a crowded room. And there was no man at her side. "Your husband have a handkerchief I could use? I need something for a blindfold—nothing big, nothing heavy."

"I don't have a husband or a handkerchief, but I do have some nice clean rags around here. I'll find something...."

When she bent over an old metal cupboard, he found himself scowling at her. She *had* to be married. All the women her age were married in this part of the country. That wasn't sexist thinking but practicality. The life-style was hard and physical. Winters, a body could be snowed in for weeks at a time. Tanner thrived on solitude and isolation, but he couldn't imagine a woman choosing that kind of life. Not a reasonably young woman, no matter what she looked like.

Her supply room was too small for two people trying to move at the same time. She bumped his arm once, brushed against his wrist. Both contacts were accidental, and no matter how naturally she kept talking, both contacts made color shoot to her cheeks.

Not that he wanted to get away from her, but...he wanted to get away from her. "I've got everything I need. You can go back to your house."

"You might think of something else when you're upstairs."

"Then I'll find it. The owl's nervous enough around me. Two of us will just make that worse."

As if she didn't hear him, she clicked her fingers. "You need a lantern. There's barely any light upstairs. And I just remembered where my dad stored the water trays for his pigeons.''

He couldn't get rid of her. Climbing back up the stairs, he had his arms full of supplies for George. Bouncing behind him, so did Charly. He couldn't force the woman to leave her own property, but he wished she would. He wasn't used to people being friendly toward him, especially women, and he was close to being mean tired. He didn't want to take that out on her, but he was out of patience, out of energy.

At least she had the good sense to stay outside the cage when he slipped inside and latched the door. His gaze and direction then became concentrated solely on his Snowy. The bird fluffed at the scent of him, and its round gold eyes opened, looking so fierce, so wild, so... vulnerable.

Tanner's expression softened a bit and he felt the rare clutch of his heart. God, it was beautiful. Why was it always the most magnificent, the most untamable, the most special of nature's creatures that ended up on the endangered species list?

"You're going to live, you know. There was no way I was ever going to let you die." As he switched on the lantern and laid out the supplies, he slowly, softly kept talking. Initially he started the conversation to reassure and calm the bird. He wasn't sure when he realized he was *really* talking to her.

"Everybody thinks of eagles and hawks and falcons as the great avian hunters. We forget about owls, when they're the best. And they've got so many strikes against them. Hawks can see by day. Owls have to find their prey at night. And an eagle can soar clear to the sun, spot her food sources for a distance of miles. An owl can't do that.''

When Tanner covered its face with the light rag, the bird shuddered, but it didn't move after that, even when its damaged wing was gently splayed. The crusted blood made the wound look worse than it was. The break was neat, just hard to work with because of the complex mass of covering feathers.

Tanner found the painkiller that Charly had tucked on the tray. He wanted to use it but didn't dare. The owl's heartbeat was already thready; the symptoms of shock were becoming a serious threat. Like too damn much in life, kindness had to take the form of cruelty. He couldn't help the bird without hurting it.

''An owl can fly, he can glide, but you'll never see one soar very high because he can't. Nature made him differently. All birds have stiff wing feathers except for the owl. His soft feathers make it possible for him to near his prey without making a sound—they also make him uniquely beautiful—but their disadvantage is strength. There's no power in softness. An owl can never soar, can never touch sky.''

He didn't splint the break, just smeared on antiseptic cream and firmly taped the whole wing in a closed position. Beneath his hands, he could feel the bird's body warmth, its fragility. Beneath all those feathers, it was incredibly small. Tanner could have sworn that nothing moved him anymore. But the owl did. The bird's heart was huge, not in size but in courage, pride, strength and will.

His expression as fierce as his touch was tender, Tanner started wrapping a thick gauze sling around the whole thing. The sling would give the owl something to peck at. George was *not* going to like the tape beneath it.

"He's the best of hunters, fearless, smart. He has to be. He picks the lonely country, the desolate territories, so he's stuck scavenging for the prey nobody else wants, nobody else is looking for. He'll take on something twice his weight and never think twice, especially where his young are concerned. When it comes to protecting his family, an owl will never back down."

The wing was done, but while the owl was still blindfolded Tanner needed to rig up a rope tether. The project was simple, yet for three short seconds it seemed insurmountable. The hammer of exhaustion beat at his temples. He'd pushed too hard, too long, and strength was ebbing out of him.

"How did you come to know so much about owls?"

They were the first words Charly had spoken to him in quite a while, and they acted like a brace. He needed one. He stiffened and forced his eyes wide. "Had a pet hoot owl as a kid. The rest—I don't know. I just picked up information along the way."

"How long do you think before the wing's healed?"

Carefully he knotted a thin rope to the bird's leg and then to the perch. "A month? Six weeks? And the timing's more complicated because it's early December. Even when the wing's healed, I'm not sure it would be wise to free him in the dead of a Minnesota winter."

"I still have the filled water container out here if you want it—"

"I'll get it." He did, furious with himself that he hadn't remembered it.

"You're good with him," she said softly.

He refused the compliment. "He's weak as hell because of me, chasing him all over the countryside." The truth of that was obvious when Tanner removed the owl's blindfold. George stayed still, trembling, the spirit to fight gone. His eyes were closed. The idea that he could still die tore at Tanner.

"He's weak because he was hurt," Charly corrected him. "He would have died if he couldn't fly, couldn't hunt. You saved his life."

Tanner whipped his eyes toward her. "Don't make me into some kind of hero. He'd probably be better off if I'd left him alone. The break wasn't that bad, and some critters just don't survive in captivity. They lose their will to live. They fret and won't eat. For all I know, I've hurt him more than helped him."

"Do you always beat yourself over the head for doing something nice? He had no chance in the wild. You gave him one. That's more than most people would do. Enough of this. Just leave the tray and all that stuff outside the cage. I'll take care of it later. You're obviously dead on your feet. The house has a spare bedroom. Before you rest I'll make you some breakfast, and then we'd better take care of that hand of yours. He really clawed you, didn't he? And your cheek—"

Before her Minnesota hospitality reached epic proportions, Tanner cut her off. "I'll be off your property in fifteen minutes. With the bird. When I'm putting this stuff away downstairs in your supply room, I'll take that mug of coffee you offered. But that's all."

He'd intimidated tree-size men when he used that tone of voice; it had no effect on her. She simply tilted her chin up and raised one pale eyebrow, studying him as if he were the recalcitrant puppy in the litter. "You're weaving on your feet and you can't keep your eyes open, Mr. Tanner—"

"*Tanner.* Not Mr. Tanner."

"And not Carson?"

"Nobody calls me Carson." He was named after a father he wanted no association with, but that was old buried history. Who cared? He wasn't even sure why he'd snapped at her about the name except that his head was pounding and he couldn't think.

"Well, Tanner, you're not leaving here in the shape you're in, so why don't you just stash that chip on your shoulder and relax." She moved toward the stairs. "If you want to put that stuff away, feel free. By that time I'll have some steak and eggs going."

"I'm not staying."

"I'm not going to waste my time arguing with a brick wall," she called over her shoulder. "Your rifle and snowshoes will be thawing in my kitchen."

"Don't touch my gun—"

"When you first come in, there's a little anteroom where you can wash your hands."

"Dammit! I'm not staying!"

"We'll see."

He barely heard the last two words; she was already out of sight. For a moment he stared down the empty stairs, unsure if he was feeling more amused or annoyed. When he was a kid, his mother used to say "we'll see" in just that way. "We'll see" always meant "we'll do it my way."

Charly's similarity to his mother scraped his sense of humor, but not for long. She distinctly wasn't his mother and he wasn't a kid but a thirty-seven-year-old two-hundred-pound man with an unsavory reputation for trouble. A man people didn't trust, a man people avoided, a man strangers were afraid of. For good reasons.

She'd recognized his name; she should have been wary of inviting him into her kitchen. Maybe he was dead beat, but he'd been dead beat before. The best thing he could do for both of them was clean up his messes, collect his owl and clear off her property. From long practice, he knew he could obliterate any trace of evidence that he'd even been here.

That was the best option, and he intended to take it.

Fifteen minutes later, he was forced to change his mind.

Two

———

"Where is my rifle?"

Although she certainly recognized a man's furious voice when she heard one, Charly never looked up from the cast-iron frying pan. "Propped next to your chair over there. Fair warning, though. You stomp in here with snowy feet and I'll use it on you."

She heard silence—a long silence—from the back hall. Then she heard a thud of one boot on the linoleum floor, followed by a second thud. A four-year-old in a tantrum wouldn't have made half the noise. She turned over the crisp side of the fried potatoes, added salt and carefully erased her smile when he loomed in her doorway.

More temper. His legs were spread and his hands hooked on his hips. With those fierce silver eyes and railroad-tie shoulders, her stranger looked as sweet as grizzled meat.

"Lady, you have one hell of a nerve."

"Tanner?"

"What?"

"Shut up and sit down," she said cheerfully.

She could see he didn't want or intend to—he'd come in for his rifle, not food—but something made him waiver. Maybe the smell of rose-cherry jam and fresh coffee? And like a moth to a flame, his gaze was drawn to the potatoes and steaks on the stove. Then to her.

Head down, she just kept pushing the spatula. It wouldn't take him long to make up his mind about her; it never took men long to make up their minds about Charly. "You want it to go to waste? Because I can't eat more than half of this," she said finally.

"I never wanted you to go to this trouble."

"Why don't you worry about it while you're washing your hands?"

By the time he'd cleaned himself up and stashed his gun and parka in the back hall, she was waiting for him with the red enameled coffeepot. Once he sat down, she filled his cup, and sneaked a good look at him.

A woman who lived in a man's country learned young when a man was at the end of his tether. Exhaustion didn't excuse bad manners, but at least it explained them. Tanner's eyes were circled and glazed; he was tired to the point of stumbling. His hands were red from cold and his cheeks burned from overexposure.

At his worst, he was a magnificent-looking man. His chamois shirt and doe-hide vest showed off the powerful stretch of his chest and shoulders. Worn jeans molded long, long thighs. He moved as if his whole body were a polished muscle and he walked like a mountain cat, lithe, sure and soundless. From the neck down, he was one sexy dangerous package.

From the neck up, he was even more lethal. His eyes were a smoked silver, light, deep-set and as wild and lonely as the north wind. His straight hair was a rich thick sable with a hint of salt. He had a king's face with all the regalness, the power, the authority that went with royalty. Nobody had ever broken that nose. Nobody had dared.

If he was still spring young, he would be daredevil handsome. Charly could picture him brash, bold, cocky and too darn good-looking for his own good. Still, he'd lost the look of a boy a long time ago. The years had hardened his features and etched some hard-living crow's-feet around his eyes. He'd known pain. He'd mastered it. Age had honed a vitality and inescapable masculinity in every clean strong line. He was a loner and a fighter and it showed.

What didn't show was what he looked like when he smiled. She hadn't seen a smile yet, and she wasn't looking forward to it. The look of him now was enough to make her knees knock, her heart hiccup, her feet trip. Not that he would have noticed that. Like the efficient practical woman she was, she smoothly set the plate in front of him.

"I'll pay you for the meal," he said gruffly.

She pushed the salt and pepper shakers where he could reach them, thinking that he had a voice like rust...and a mouth that must have caused a lot of women trouble. "If the only thing you've got to say is nonsense, you'd do well to keep quiet. I can make a horse stampede when I get in a good temper, and believe me, you're pushing it."

She almost—*almost*—had that smile. But then he bent his head and gave his full attention to the plate. Gentleman's manners notwithstanding, he had the hunger of a starved wolf. "I thought you were going to eat, too."

"I already had breakfast." She'd moved to the sink to put the two pans in soapy water to soak. She hated dishes to begin with, and there was nothing worse than cleaning dried eggs. "Did you check your gun for harm? I mean...I didn't contaminate it with perfume or cooties or anything by just carrying it in the house, did I?"

He kept his eyes on her. "I may be a little oversensitive about people touching my rifle."

"No kidding!" She swiped the crumbs from the red-tiled counter, closed a cupboard and drawer—she liked her kitchen neat—then poured herself a mug of coffee. "Eggs too done for you?"

"They're fine." He cleared his throat and added gruffly, "Not fine. Great. Thank you."

"You lie like a rug. The whole county knows I cook eggs tougher than old leather."

He nearly choked and then grappled with the sudden silence. "The steak's perfect."

She said demurely, "I know," and finally won his smile. Not a big parade, no fanfare, but the curve of his lips stole the harshness from his features, added the sting of sensuality. She dropped into the chair at the opposite end of the long pine table. Red-and-white checked curtains blocked the blustery gloom of a December morning; the hanging lamp overhead provided a cheerful bright glow. Wrapping her hands around her mug, she watched him eat and tried to fathom the mystery of Carson Tanner.

She lived in the stretch of border country west of International Falls and knew that Tanner had grown up some fifteen miles east of her family's place. She also knew that his father had split when his son was young, that his mother had run a small ranch alone and that Carson had left the area after high school to take a job with U.S. Customs. Mrs. Tanner had died three years ago of pneumonia while Carson seemed to be living out a "local boy makes good" story. He'd been with Customs a total of eighteen years, rose in the ranks and traveled in the process to places like San Francisco, Miami and New York.

Charly didn't know all that by choice but chance. Winters were tediously long and neighbors sparse and few between. If a mouse breathed, it was grist for the gossip mill. She'd never met Tanner before. His family had just been part of the local news circuit like everyone else.

The mystery about Tanner began when he came home a year ago. Some said he'd "retired." At his young age that was a clear-cut euphemism for being fired. All anyone really knew was that he'd left Customs fast and under a suspicious cloud, like a maverick stallion leaving dust in its wake.

He'd set up house in the old Tanner homestead, but he wasn't ranching anything beyond a few acres of wheat. He owned a seaplane, but he didn't seem to use that as a source of business. He occasionally joined a search-and-rescue team in the parks—both Voyageurs and the Boundary Waters Canoe Area were just east of International Falls—but that was volunteer work, no pay. Lack of an income didn't seem to worry him. That he wasn't making many friends didn't seem to worry him, either.

It was hard *not* to make friends in northern Minnesota. Not that Charly was prejudiced, but northern Minnesotans were probably the friendliest people on earth. Also the loneliest. All you had to do was talk and they'd probably forgive a body any mistake. Tanner didn't talk. He gave no one a reason to dislike him, but his seclusion had gradually fostered wariness and worry. People were just a little scared of Carson Tanner. He didn't do anything to make them change their minds.

Charly had a long streak of caution and kept telling herself that she should feel fear, too, but she didn't. Maybe he was tough, maybe he was dangerous, maybe he was the bad news everyone said . . . but "everyone" hadn't seen him with that owl. He'd tended the bird with the patience and tenderness of a father with a newborn. She'd never seen gentler hands. She'd never seen more compassionate eyes.

And beyond that, fear rarely affected her reaction to a man. Why should it? She'd been capably handling men all her life, using her private and infallible set of rules. When a man was hungry, you fed him. When a man was tired, you offered him a bed. And when a man was ornery, you gave him a little rope and then you politely made him behave.

Tanner was currently behaving just fine, and he was on his last bite of toast and last forkful of potatoes. Hunger had obviously added to his sharp edge. Sated now, he simply looked worn and weary, but the glances he kept shooting her were careful, like a man who never forgot to watch his back. Charly had never made a man nervous in her life. The idea amused her.

Thoughtfully she got up one more time to refill his coffee. "So, what are we going to feed our owl, Tanner?"

His mug locked halfway to his mouth when she said "our," but he answered the question. "In the wild, he'll eat mostly rodents—rats, mice, shrews. Small reptiles in the summer. Maybe a rabbit. You live here alone?"

He tacked that on as if it had been bothering him. She nodded. "My parents retired to Arizona about three years ago. Dad had a small lung problem, and the winters had simply gotten too much for both of them."

"You weren't tempted to move with them?"

"My Belgians like the cold. I doubt they would have been fond of Arizona's heat. My parents didn't need me, and everything else that mattered to me was here—the horses, the land, friends. This was home." She added, "I'd like to keep him for you."

Tanner was rubbing his temple so hard he was making dents. He abruptly stopped. "Keep him?"

"George. It seems logical. I have traps set all over the barn for mice, so it shouldn't be hard to keep him fed. You're probably not set up with a cage, are you? Where I already have the coop and he's settled in it.

Also, I know your place must be around fifteen miles from here—''

''That has nothing to do with the owl.''

''Sure it does. He's injured, vulnerable. Maybe he's used to the cold, but it doesn't seem a very good idea to add more stress by carting him cross-country. Why do it? I'm here every day and I wouldn't mind taking care of him.''

Tanner sliced in, ''No. He'd bite your head off the minute you stepped in the cage. He'll only be physically weak for a few days' time. He's not going to like that bandage and he's not going to like finding himself in captivity.''

''I've handled wild critters before.''

''You won't have to worry about handling him. I'm taking him with me. Thank you for the offer, but no.''

''You're not thinking reasonably. You're too tired,'' she said mildly.

He didn't like the comment. He liked it even less when she rose to rummage in a back cupboard and returned with a first-aid kit. ''Put your hand on the table,'' she said.

Instead, he just looked at her in a way that made her feel as hot as if she'd eaten a jalapeño pepper. There was nothing sensual or sexual in his eyes. There never was when a man looked at her. But he had a force in those gray-silver eyes, a magnetism that clearly registered a lamb should be smarter than to push a wolf.

Charly was duly impressed, but she'd never been much of a lamb. ''I have a choice of chocolate chip cookies or Oreos for dessert. You get neither unless you put your hand on the table,'' she said severely. From the set of his jaw, she got the definite impression that few people had the nerve to order him around, much less tease him.

Pity, because the most gravelly sound came out of his throat and his right hand slid on the table. "You browbeat every stranger you meet, or is it just me?" he asked dryly.

"Everyone. I'm not selective." She set out tape, gauze, scissors and cream, then slid her palm under his to hold his hand steady. "This is real pretty, Tanner. I hate to think how deep the gouge would have been if you hadn't been wearing gloves." His palm was life warm, calloused, hard. Touching him sent a lustful spiral of heat through her bloodstream, which she ignored. All her life she'd had a rampantly romantic imagination. Ignoring it was one of her most practiced skills.

"This isn't going to hurt. I never bought the philosophy about no pain, no gain, and the cream's an antibiotic. You'd better take the tube with you if you don't have some at home. Use it again tomorrow, and change the bandage. Animal scratches are nothing to fool around with."

"Thank you, Miss Nag."

She chuckled. As she released his hand, though, she remembered the shallow scratch near his right jawline. When he saw where she was looking, he said a firm "no."

"Do you have to argue about everything, Tanner? Tilt your face."

When he didn't, she nudged his chin up with her thumb and leaned over him. The scratch on his cheek was only superficial, but an animal scratch was still an animal scratch. When she smoothed on the cream, she felt the bristle of whiskers under her fingertips and saw his steady gaze. Again she felt a bolt of sexual awarenesss, unwanted, inappropriate and, this time, upsetting. Nothing wrong with a little imagination, a little fantasy. But she'd die if he guessed her feelings.

"There. Done." She moved back quickly and busied herself with reboxing the first-aid supplies. "You'll be thrilled to hear I'm only going to nag you about one more thing. From the look of you, you've been up all night and then some. Until the roads are cleared, I can't offer to drive you home, but your taking off on foot in this weather without some rest first strikes me as just plain stupid. There's four bedrooms in this house. You have a choice of three."

"No, thank you."

She expected his refusal and paid no attention. After storing the first-aid box, she aimed for the dishes. "Where I come from, Tanner, we don't send basket cases back out in the cold. I've put up stray dogs and I've put up strangers. I put up a tiger cat once and got stuck with an entire litter of kittens on my favorite chair, and I've put up a moose who was so damned starved and cold he was driven to the shelter of the barn—"

"Charly—"

"And a very long time ago, I put up a snowmobiler—an extremely egotistical man, a tourist, who totally misunderstood Minnesotan concepts of hospitality. Truthfully, he kind of tickled my sense of humor. Most men take a look at me and never get those kinds of ideas. Regardless, he was one thing. You're another. You're from around here, so you're not about to misunderstand a basic offer of hospitality, and somewhere in that thick skull you have to have a brain. You're dead on your feet.''

''I just had coffee.''

''If you're counting on caffeine, don't. I made decaf.'' She heard the way his words were starting to blur. ''And if you'll give it a chance, I think you'll find the meal was its own sleeping pill.''

''I'm not staying.''

She nodded. ''First bedroom off the hall to the left is a spare. Bathroom across from it. Pipes scream when you turn on the hot water, but everything works. Pillow and comforter are down, and I'll check on your owl.'' She picked up his plate and silverware and turned toward the sink.

''Charly, I can't stay.''

The words came out as thick as a drunk's. Charly, silent, just kept wiping a pan.

She never looked up when she heard his chair scrape back. She could feel the glare of his eyes on her back, figured he'd *really* like to lash out at something right now—preferably her—but he didn't. When she finally risked a peek, she saw him stumbling through her living room toward the hall.

She smiled faintly, but not for long. There was nothing humorous about a man who'd driven himself so hard and so close to the breaking point that he couldn't think, couldn't argue, couldn't see. Maybe the owl mattered that much to him. Or maybe he lived his whole life that way.

She finished the dishes and then dressed up for the winter windchill. She had stalls to clean and her Belgians to groom and exercise.

A half hour later she had two stalls finished and all the horses in the east pasture but Blitzen. When she opened his stall, he made a good show of hoof-stomping, teeth-baring temper. Blitz weighed a solid 2200 pounds, had breeding lines that could rival that of the Prince of Wales, could service seventy-five mares in season without overexerting himself and, God help her, was the meanest stallion she'd ever had. She'd half sold her soul to own the devil, and when push had come to shove, she'd forgotten his breeding lines. She'd loved him on sight. Still did.

She slapped his handsome rump hard and, once he was freed in the pasture, returned to face a wheelbarrow full of manure and another hour with a pitchfork. After that came dosing out worm paste, followed by hoof-cleaning time. She thought wryly that it was not a glamorous life.

At eighteen she'd known the breeding lines she wanted, and her father had given her one good mare. She'd bred the mare, then traded both the mare and her colt for her first stallion of real quality. Fourteen years later she had three blue-ribbon stallions for stud, four pregnant mares, another waiting for the season, and three colts and a filly to sell this spring.

As stud farms went, hers was small. Charly had never wanted a big operation. She'd just wanted to be best, and this way she only needed outside help during the breeding and summer seasons. That was always what she'd wanted—to make it alone, in her own way and on her own terms.

This way, no one on earth had to know she made lace in her spare time. Or that she grew orchids in her minigreenhouse in the winter. Or that she read wild erotic romances or wore satin next to her skin, which was the silliest of all. Charly had always known she was plain.

She had no fear of hard work, no fear of challenge or solitude or risk. When it came down to it, there was only one thing she had ever been afraid of, and that was making a fool of herself with a man.

Charly had escaped beauty—heck, she'd also escaped pretty, cute, lovely and that whole raft of feminine adjectives. But nature had equipped her with enough pride for ten women. She didn't mind curling her fingers on the wooden rungs of a wheelbarrow full of manure. But dwelling on the feel of Tanner's warm calloused hand in her own—no. Maybe she was stuck with a romantic imagination, but she had enough pride to nip it.

He wasn't for her.

Tanner woke with a bolt. Blood pounding in his ears, he automatically reached for the rifle at his side. Instead of a gun, his hand groped over a slick soft comforter, and he could have sworn he smelled roses.

The room was pitch-dark. It took him a minute to place the sensations, the textures, the scents. In time, the adrenaline stopped pumping. There was no danger here, no threat, no enemy.

Just a woman named Charly Erickson somewhere in the house and, directly in the room, an old-fashioned alarm clock with a luminous dial that read ten. He didn't believe the time. There was no chance he'd slept fourteen hours. He never slept more than five, and then always lightly, always half awake, half aware, ready.

Abruptly he swung his legs over the side of the bed. He wouldn't have put it past Charly to have hit him with a stone to knock him out. That's how he felt: knocked out, sluggish and stiff from sleeping in his clothes. Before getting up, he rubbed at the nagging cramp in his right thigh. Years ago, a doctor had told him that the knife wound had severed a few nerves. Tanner wished it had severed a few more.

Once up, he moved silently to the door. When he crossed the hall to the bathroom, he heard no sounds, but that was logical. Ranchers bedded down early. He hoped she did.

He splashed his face with cold water because she'd said the hot made a noise. His beard needed a shave, which could wait, but his teeth couldn't. He wasn't about to borrow her toothbrush, but a little toothpaste on his finger wouldn't hurt.

He didn't find the toothpaste until he opened the medicine cabinet. The rest of the bathroom was utilitarian, blue and white tiles, blue towels and rug, no sign of a woman's trappings. Inside her medicine cabinet, though, was one shelf full of tiny perfume bottles—crystal bubbles and delicate flacons and fragile teardrops.

Rubbing the paste on his teeth, he couldn't stop looking at them. There was nothing surprising about a woman liking perfume, but that she kept her "pretties" out of sight bothered him. And kept bothering him.

By the time he was striding—silently—through her dark living room toward the kitchen, a frown was wedged on his forehead. The woman bothered him, period. Living alone on the edge of nowhere! Feeding total strangers! Allowing an unknown man to sleep in her house! For all she knew he could be a thief and a rapist. His reputation had pegged him for everything else.

She'd pinned a note on the door leading to the back hall: "Tanner—Sandwich in fridge. Cookies in cupboard over the sink."

Still scowling, he reached for the three-decker sandwich and then rifled through her cupboard, ignoring the homemade chocolate chips, reaching for the Oreos. Damn woman. It was as if she knew. He survived an annual bout of hypothermia. His body was used to punishment, his needs were few—but in this life he could not survive for long without Oreos.

With two in his mouth, he followed the trail of wood scent to her basement door. Below, as expected from the smell, he found a wood furnace. Three days' supply of wood was neatly stacked and she had a room with an old-fashioned coal bin where loose logs had been piled helter-skelter. He pulled off his vest and shirt and worked up a sweat. That took a longer time than he had. Hell, he had *no* time, not after sleeping fourteen hours—but he could hardly do less. She'd fed and put him up. He owed her.

By midnight he was striding toward her barn, carrying his snowshoes and rifle. His boots made scrunching sounds in the two inches of new snow and the wind tried to take his head off. He heard the crazed howl of a gray wolf when he pulled open the barn door, which was when he discovered the light left on inside.

A yearling poked her head from the stall and made a soft snuffling sound. The young one seemed to assume that anyone who passed would want to pet her. Time or no time, he paused to stroke her nose but abruptly stopped, bracing himself, when he heard a sound.

He heard it again, a crooning, a faint drifting music. Silent as a cougar, he climbed the first stair to the loft and then another. Halfway up, his head was even with the second floor. From the battery lantern hung on a hook, he saw his owl, his beautiful Snowy with its bandaged wing and its yellow-gold eyes staring out. And he saw Charly sitting cross-legged on the bare wooden floor. She wasn't doing anything but sitting there. Singing the owl love songs.

For a moment he pinched the flesh between his eyes with two fingers. Twelve o'clock at night with wolves on the prowl and she was singing torch songs to a solemn-faced owl.

"Charly? What are you doing here?"

When her head whipped around, Tanner remembered the exact reason he'd been in such an all-fired hurry to escape the house. He just *really* didn't want to see her look at him that way again. He would have known what to do with a woman's flirting smile, a come-on, the body language of invitation—all the things a woman did to announce she was available.

Charly didn't do any of that. The coat hugged around her was a man's shapeless jacket. She wore none of the makeup that might have softened the angular lines of her face. Everything about her said who she was—a strong practical woman without vanity, a woman content with her choices. Those eyes simply said something else. Her soft green eyes were touched with shy yearning, a guileless vulnerable confession

that she found him attractive. He doubted—he
knew—she didn't intend him to see. But he did. And
he didn't know what to do about it.

Her cheeks flushed bronze by lantern light—she'd
never intended to be caught singing—but she re-
covered her sense of humor almost immediately, mo-
tioning toward the owl. "He was all upset, trying to
peck off the sling. I had to do something. Would you
believe he likes Whitney Houston and Rodgers and
Hammerstein? But he's not real fond of country."

"Fussy, is he?" Tanner asked dryly, but his eyes
narrowed when he looked in the coop. "Want to tell
me how the dead mouse got in there?"

"I checked the traps downstairs. It was fresh, and I
thought—"

"You didn't think. You weren't supposed to go
anywhere near him."

"How else could I show you that I could handle
him? He didn't hurt me. Didn't try." She looked at
him critically. "You had a good rest and it shows, so
now let's try talking sense. I know you formed a bond
with the owl, which is certainly easy to understand—"

"I beg your pardon?"

"You're alike, Tanner. Surely you can see that?"
When he responded with a perplexed frown, she simply went on. "Never mind. The point is that bond or
not, I doubt that it can be very easy for you to take
him with you. The best choice is obviously for him to
stay here. You tell me what to do for him, I'll do it.
You can visit him whenever you please. It's your owl.
But with your work—"

"Slow down." His body had turned razor tense, spring tight. What she said was absolutely true, but she couldn't know it. He climbed the rest of the stairs and hunkered down beside her where he had a clearer view of her face. He knew his voice came out harsh. "You seem to have jumped to a lot of conclusions from nowhere. What did you mean, 'with my work'?"

"Just what I said."

"Anyone in the county can tell you that I'm not employed."

"I'm well aware of that," Charly said patiently.

"And if you've heard that, you've heard that I was fired from Customs after eighteen years. They don't fire you from the service for nothing after all that time. Some say it was for drugs, some say for smuggling contraband."

"Some say," she agreed. "Now about the owl—"

"To hell with the owl. If you'd heard all that, I'll be damned if I can understand why you invited me in your house. And I'm telling you right now that the rumors are all true."

She didn't even hesitate. "And horses fly."

"I was fired for misconduct."

"I don't think so."

His jaw locked. "And I am not employed."

"I'm quite sure you are. At what, I have no idea. Nor have I asked, have you noticed? It's not my business. Why don't we drop this subject? It's obviously making you uncomfortable. About your owl..."

He, too, was thinking about the owl. He could have told her that when threatened, a male Great Snowy aggressively flapped its wings. The classic threat display was a defense, a way of successfully warning off predators twice its size.

When he reached for Charly, his instinct was just as primal, just as basic. She startled when his arm swept around her, when he jutted her chin up with his knuckles and slammed his mouth on hers. To hurt her was never a motivation. Heck, he'd lose a limb before hurting a woman, but to scare Charly was something else. He knew how she'd looked at him, and she needed a good scaring. Enough so that she wouldn't take in the next stranger quite so trustingly, wouldn't feed them perfect steaks quite so willingly, wouldn't wildly assume their innocence... quite so blindly.

His fingers clutched in her hair, tight enough that he heard the ping of a rubber band, and suddenly her braid loosened. Her hair feathered around his hands, fine hair, silky, the kind that never behaved well on a woman's terms, but Tanner was not a woman. The soft strands slid through his fingers and he felt his heartbeat thunder in his ears. She smelled like roses, and the panicky stiffness he expected from her mouth wasn't there. The darn woman didn't have an ounce of self-preservation in her makeup. She invited too much. Too willingly. Too... simply.

Charly never tensed. She just went still. Her eyes closed and her throat arched and her lips yielded under his in lush invitation.

And an angry, angry kiss changed immutably to something else. He hadn't come this close to a woman's softness in years. He didn't have the right, not with his work and life-style, but the wound of loneliness ached now like a wolf's howl, a hound's baying, an owl's lonely hoot.

In the silence, in the shadows, his thumb brushed her cheek and his lips touched hers again, softly now. Her mouth was tender, mobile, trembly. She knew nothing. The feel of a man's hard thighs against hers was enough to make her shudder. Layers of material separated them. He could still feel her heart pound.

When he first tasted her tongue, she reacted virgin shy, uneasy...and then sweet, like something he'd lost. Luring and wild, like something he'd forgotten. Her hands never climbed as far as his neck but they reached his upper arms and she clutched, and he tasted the silk of passion. Like something he had no right to.

He pulled back, abruptly and hard. Charly's arms were left in midair, her eyes dazed and vulnerable. He could tell that she'd never planned her response.

But, dammit, neither had he.

"Don't you have any sense, woman?" he said harshly. "You're alone on this place. You don't know me from Adam. When a stranger comes on to you like that, you've got every right to knock him clear across the room!"

She never answered. He hardly gave her the chance. Disturbed, furious, he lurched to his feet, spared one last long look at his owl and headed for the stairs.

Below, he strapped on his snowshoes, hefted his rifle and headed out into the night. Snow stung his face. The black ominous clouds matched his temper; the wind whipped and blew. He wasn't sure if he was madder at her—or himself.

It hardly mattered.

He wouldn't be back.

Three

———

It's been two days, George. You have to be hungry."
Charly suspended the field mouse from her gloved
hand. "Isn't he pretty? Doesn't he look tasty?" Her
voice lowered to a whisper. "Couldn't you at least
look at him? Please?"

George's eyes fixed coldly and unwaveringly on her
face as if the mouse didn't exist. Finally giving in,
Charly turned her head to drop the meal in the owl's
food dish, which was a mistake. Although her head
was only averted for seconds, it was enough time for
the Snowy to skitter sideways on its perch and sink its
sharp beak into her shoulder.

She froze. "We've been through this before,
George."

If she turned at all, the owl's beak would be in
pecking range of her eyes or face. If she tried to pull

away, the injured bird could become unbalanced and fall or choose to grasp her braid instead of her jacket. They'd been through that yesterday. She'd lost a handful of hair in the encounter. How could she have been so stupid as to turn her back again?

"You have a serious problem with hostility, George. Very serious. Hasn't anyone ever told you that you lose all your brownie points when you bite the hand that feeds you? You're going to get another long lecture in manners if you don't watch it."

George didn't care. He had the human pinned and nervous. His favorite game in town. Charly sighed.

For two days she'd wooed him, talked to him, sung and cared for him. That wasn't such a long time, but she was making no headway at all. The bird wasn't eating, and Charly was afraid he wasn't going to. He simply didn't want to live caged, and his rage was blind, those gold eyes awesome, filled with such vulnerable anger... such bullheaded pride.

He reminded her of Tanner.

In time, the owl tired of the game and loosened its beak from her shoulder. With less grace than speed, Charly sprang free, turning only when she was well out of pecking range. And then she looked at the Snowy. The big bandage on its wing wouldn't hold out much longer; George hadn't been able to reach the tape, but he'd all but shredded the sling. His big yellow eyes had lost their luster. The bird was weak, but even now his chest was defiantly puffed, his head regal, his posture proud and his white cloak of feathers as magnificent as a king's cape.

Lord, you're beautiful. Just like him. She blindly reached for the white cloth from the first-aid tray on the floor. Another day and he'd be at the tape if she couldn't rebandage the wing. She'd watched Tanner and she knew what to do. Slower than slow motion, more gentle than cottondown, she raised the white cloth she intended to use as a blindfold.

In the snap of a second, he grabbed it and attacked. What his talons didn't rip, his beak tore and shredded. Bits of white flew. By the time the dust settled, he was glaring at her again.

"Well, you killed another rag. Congratulations," she said dryly, but she couldn't hold the humor. "You're hurting, dammit, and you know darn well I'm not your enemy. *Why* won't you let me help you?"

Below, she could hear an occasional whicker and snuffle. Her Belgians wanted exercise. And in the supply room, her scarred desk was cluttered with tack hammers and horse liniment and bridle rings and, somewhere, the horror of tax forms that came with December. She couldn't stand there and argue with a stubborn owl.

But she couldn't seem to make herself leave. She kept looking at the bird and seeing Tanner. The same thing had happened more than once over the past two days. Unbidden, unwanted, Tanner's face would suddenly prowl through her mind like a silent stalking cat, ever there, waiting, pouncing when she was least prepared.

Just like his owl, Tanner mistrusted kindness. She'd offered nothing more than a little human warmth, and he'd turned on her. Initially his kiss had contained no desire. He'd come at her with the clear-cut intention of shaking her up and scaring her off.

He was successful. The pass had scared her plenty, but not because she was afraid of Tanner. Her own response had shaken her then, and the memory of it was still shaking her now. Poor man. The last thing he must have expected was her draping herself all over him, awkward as a rug. She could imagine what he thought. The classic spinster living alone, man starved and lonesome.

The image always made her cringe. Most stereotypes were cruel precisely for the elements of truth they contained. She *was* alone and, at thirty-two, qualified as a seasoned spinster—at least in these parts. Her lack of good looks was undeniable. There were days her hormones sang in physical need for a man, and yes, she was lonely.

She didn't, though, come on like white water rapids to any male stranger she could trip and strip at the door. In fact, Charly had banished her lonesome hormones to a mental attic a long time ago, exactly so something like this couldn't happen. Lonesome was livable; giving a man something to laugh at was not. The men she knew respected her for her independence, her strength, her skills, her grit. She wanted that respect. She'd earned it. To let on that she was a closet romantic, that she dreamed of sheikhs and knights and blue silk and passion...

Good Lord. They'd take one look at her and laugh her off the block.

Charly had always been extraordinarily careful with men until two nights ago. She could have coped with the renegade aggressive streak in Tanner. Hell's bells, if she could make a two-thousand-pound horse behave, she could certainly hold her own with a man.

She had held her own just fine, until the exact moment when the chill in his eyes had changed to raw hunger. The exact moment when he'd swept those big arms around her, and he'd shuddered, and she'd felt the blind lonely rub of his mouth on hers, the seeking, the need, the wildness like an explosion. . . .

He'd kissed her like a man who could break. Like a man who would break if he couldn't hold on to someone.

And every defense she'd ever built had folded like a house of cards.

Charly irritably pushed her hands through her hair. *We know that, Charly. He knows it, too, and since he hasn't been back here in two days—even for his owl— that pretty much says it all. You embarrassed the bits out of him.*

Hands on hips, she narrowed her eyes on George, who, par for the course, was staring at her with his usual "dare you" belligerence. "You're just dying for me to try and come close again, aren't you? You don't really want me anywhere near you." She let herself out of the cage and latched the door. "Tough luck, George," she whispered softly. "I'm going to help you whether you like it or not. You can sharpen that beak all day, but tonight I'm fixing that wing. And you eat that damn mouse or I'm going to shoot you!"

Outside, the wind was hurling a sheet of snow on the iced-over river. Tanner, standing at the window, felt angry for no reason. Impatient for no reason. The restless mood had been eating at him for two days. *Damn fool woman.*

It would never happen again, but that resolution failed to banish Charly from his mind. He kept recalling things, like the pulse of her throat under his fingertips, like her quicksilver responsiveness. Her lips had the texture of newness; they'd trembled under his. She'd known as much about kissing as an untried girl, which hadn't stopped her from turning his head inside out. Tanner never lost his head; it was *her*. She'd been so damned warm, so damned willing, so damned...sweet.

He wasn't going back there, but that didn't stop the woman from haunting him. What if it had been someone else up in that hayloft with her? Another man? How lonely was she? How many men knew she lived alone?

Probably the whole county.

"Tanner, I know this is asking a lot, but is there some remote chance I could woo you away from that window and get you to sit down and listen?"

Tanner stiffened, then turned with a dry glance for his boss. "I was listening. I always listen to you, Evan."

"When you're in the mood, yes. When you agree with what I say, yes. It's just a pity that both occasions happen so rarely, and you're looking like holy hell. If I didn't know you so well, I'd be worried about you."

"Don't waste your time."

"I won't, but sit, would you? You're making me nervous."

Tanner chuckled, forced the image of a jade-eyed woman with a sassy tongue out of his mind and obediently sprawled in the white leather chair across from

Evan's desk. In his buckskin vest and jeans, he never failed to feel like an interloper in this office. The whole room was white leather and teak and law books. It smelled like old money and suited his boss.

Evan, as always, was wearing an impeccable linen shirt and creased trousers. His build rivaled Napoleon's; he'd never reached five-four, but he had the shrewd sharp eyes of a hawk. From fluffed white hair to florid complexion and impeccable clothes, he had the look of money and breeding, education and class. No one could doubt he was a gentleman, except Tanner, who knew better.

The respect between men was absolute, but they'd perfected the game of slinging insults over the years. Neither wanted to admit they were alike, and in looks, they certainly weren't. Amused, Tanner watched his boss lay his elbows on the varnished desk and make a meticulous steeple with his fingertips. "You heard what I said about the complexities of the silver tariff? Too much silver is coming across. That's not going to get better until the change in law goes into effect."

"I heard."

"The river's frozen over early this year, adding to our problems. You can already drive across it."

"Yes."

"I told you the value of the drugs that made it to the streets of Winnipeg. The Canadians weren't happy. It's a good clean city, always has been. They don't need our trash."

"No."

Tanner's mind wandered. He thought fleetingly that a crowd of hundreds could have heard their conversation and never made sense of it. Some days he wished he didn't. Some days he wished Evan hadn't plucked him from his regular job at Customs. Actually, he had no recollection of the exact point when he'd gotten involved in an invisible job that had no title and no rules. Loyalty started and stopped here in this room. If he was ever in trouble, he knew Evan would forget his name. The chances of Tanner finding trouble were excellent. Even when he had maintained the token job title in Customs, very little he did was conventional.

No man with any sense of honor would ask a woman to share his life-style. Tanner had never done the kind of work that went with a good woman and a passel of kids and a kitchen with apple pie. Lately, though, the prices had seemed exorbitantly high for the choices he'd made. Lately he'd been wrangling with the isolation and loneliness like a rogue flu he couldn't shake.

Lately he'd met a green-eyed woman—a woman who was absolutely nothing to him and never would be. Hell, she was plain as fried potatoes without the salt. Why couldn't he forget her?

Dammit, Charly, how many strangers have you taken in in the past two days? If you were pretty, I wouldn't have to worry about you. Pretty women have a way of taking care of themselves.

His gaze focused belatedly on the shot glass hovering in front of him. "Chivas," Evan said dryly. "You won't appreciate it, but it might help. You look ready to climb the walls. I realize that's standard for you, but maybe sometime in this life you might try relaxing."

"I *am* relaxed," he protested, but he took the shot glass. The initial gulp of tawny liquid at first burned all the way down his throat, then soothed. Nothing had changed; nothing was wrong. The woman hounding his mind for the past two days was nothing to him and never could be. His work was his life, and that commitment was irreversible. That was not an issue of the ties Evan imposed on him but of the ties he imposed on himself.

Evan didn't restart the conversation until the shot glass was empty. "Seems there was a little incident at the north border of the Boundary Waters Canoe Area yesterday."

"Was there?"

"A private plane, where none was supposed to be. Had the forest people on both sides real irritated. No engines allowed in that area, of course. You wouldn't know anything about that, would you?"

"Not a thing." Evan was studying him with those shrewd hawk's eyes. Unable to sit still, Tanner lurched out of the chair.

"And then a package of drugs showed up in Baudette. Baudette, for Lord's sake. Lucky the local authorities didn't take it home and use it for sugar. They were real riled up, no way to explain the package, no markings on it, no link to anything or anybody."

"A real mystery," Tanner commented obligingly, but he'd stopped listening. Below, two hundred yards away, the Rainy River was a narrow icy ribbon.

He could see Canada across that ribbon, the distance between countries no bigger than a blink. Someone who had border property—like Charly, for instance—might as easily share morning coffee with a neighboring Canadian as an American. Why not? The friendliness of the unfenced border between the two giant nations was legend. Most people took it for granted.

Evan didn't, and neither did Tanner.

The two countries had compatible laws, compatible law enforcement agencies and damned good people on both sides who cared enough to make that friendly border work. Sometimes, though, it wasn't enough. Laws and budgets, politics and protocol all took time. Time that a smart criminal could use to his advantage. Lowlifes everywhere cuddled at geographical borders. They always had and they always would.

Tanner stared at the lost snowswept river below. Evan had bullied him into coming home the year before, claiming he'd earned a rest and less pressure. He hadn't rested yet, and the pressure never let up.

No one associated the northern Minnesota border with the immigration or drug problems such as those found in a Miami, a New York or in the Texas border towns. Population was scarce this far north, the roads few and the border notoriously peaceful. The locals would never believe there was a problem because they weren't part of it.

The same bleakness and isolation that limited population, though, was a natural boon for those who sought it. A man with a trunkful of cocaine might not be pleased about crossing the border at, say, Detroit and Windsor en route to Toronto. Authorities were everywhere at the major city crossings. But all it took was a little gas and a little time, and he could drive across the frozen Rainy River in the winter with bags of cocaine taped to his forehead. No one would notice. No one would see him.

"Tanner?"

He never looked away from the window. He never knew who paid him, but it wasn't Evan. He did know that his current salary came from both Canadian and American sources. He made a lot of money doing a job no one else wanted to do. He'd always wanted to do it. Danger had always drawn him, so had challenge and risk. Honor got smashed in there somewhere. Tanner had always had a conscience that wouldn't let him go.

Evan moved beside him and lit a thin brown cigarette from a sterling lighter. "You're thinking about quitting."

Tanner massaged the nape of his neck, unsurprised that Evan had picked up on his thoughts. Evan could read a sphinx. The skill had annoyed him for years. "Maybe," he said flatly. "It's been a lot of years. I've done my share."

"I agree. You did and you have." Evan's cool blue eyes focused on the lake. "You're tired of having to always look over your shoulder. You're tired of hunting men. You're tired of having no one to talk to, and that's been worse since I transferred you here. This is home to you. I don't think it occurred to you in eighteen years how much you valued it. Am I hitting the high points?"

Tanner stared at him. "Do you have any idea how irritating that mind-reading habit of yours is?"

Evan didn't smile. "You want some kind of life. You thought I wouldn't realize that? But you're not ready to give it up, Tanner. You may never be. A little ranch is never going to hold you." He stubbed out his cigar tip in a crystal ashtray. "I have a solution, but not one I'm willing to discuss quite yet. For now, you've put yourself in your own bind. You are where you are because you're the best at what you do. I can't replace you and I can't afford to lose you." He added the obvious. "You won't let me down."

Tanner thought wryly that his boss was a master of manipulation. When he said, 'You won't let me down,' Tanner was supposed to jump. And he did. Every time. His cage was a blend of responsibility, honor, values and conscience—but a cage was still a cage.

A fleeting image of the Great Snowy Owl passed through his mind. *George, I'll bet you're mean as hell. You wouldn't like cages any more than I do.* Tanner might have smiled if the image hadn't reminded him of Charly again. It went against every grain to leave her alone to cope with the owl, but to return was not a choice. This way, she only had to face George's claws.

If he went back there, she might have to face his. For Tanner, Charly had been a lethal exposure to what he couldn't have, couldn't want and wasn't supposed to need.

For her sake, he wasn't going back there.

"All right—out! All of you. Right now. Scoot. Vamoose."

"Come on, Charly. We just got here."

"Just got here? It's nearly nine o'clock! You drank all my coffee. You ate my whole pie—"

"A great pie, Charly."

"You've dripped snow all over my kitchen and your wives are going to wonder where you are."

"They know we're here," Lars immediately corrected her.

"Which is half the point," Charly said firmly. "Your wives owe me money for baby-sitting you big lugs." She started plucking stocking caps from the radiator and hurling them. "Any winter day too cold to work and where do you go? Charly's. Wives kick you out for being rowdy and restless and where do you go? Charly's."

"Come on, Charly. You love us. Admit it." Whitt's grin was a slash of white in a big black beard.

"I'll love you even more when you're gone. Now, whose gloves are these?"

"I think she means it this time," Howe drawled to Lars.

"See that long rectangle at the end of the hall? It's called a door. D-o-o-r. Attached to it is this little contraption called a knob. Its function is to let people go in and out. You all understand *in*. You just have to concentrate real hard on mastering the concept of *out*."

They all knew she wasn't really mad at them, so herding them out was inevitably a slow process. Curt couldn't find his hat; Whitt got started on the price of grain with Howe; Lars claimed his wife didn't feed him—which was extremely humorous, with his girth—and wouldn't leave without another brownie.

Charly grabbed a jacket, still playing shepherd, because she knew if she didn't go out with them they'd stand around and talk for another two hours.

Outside, the yard light pooled yellow on the cluster of snowmobiles. The night was bitter but clear. Two days of wind had swept the snow from the open fields, and the drifts in the yard had a crust like a sugar glaze. A pale light glinted from the narrow top window in her barn, a lonely light like a vigil. As soon as the men were gone, she could see to George.

Toes freezing, fingers cramped and cold, she waited patiently for the boys to leave. Howe finally swung a leg over his snowmobile. Whitt and Curt descended on her for a bone-crunching hug and a last tease, which was when she heard the pound of hooves. All four men turned their heads at the same time she did.

The stallion was as black as ink and coming hell-bent for leather from her north woods. She caught the glint of metal, a half-raised rifle, which was when her heart started thudding.

Her heart recognized Tanner before her eyes did. Never mind the sheepskin jacket, he could have been an avenging Indian from a century before. His stallion had the wildness and speed, and he had the look: the pride, the height, the hardness, the intensity, the power.

When he reached the edge of her yard she could see his eyes, dark as danger, darting from man to man and, as far as she could tell, deliberately avoiding her. He abruptly lowered his rifle, and just as fast, his face took on the color of windburn.

After all that thundering speed, he suddenly swung an extremely slow leg over the saddle and dismounted. His face was shadowed for a moment as he picked up the reins. Charly could see him hesitate. Then he neared her stone-still neighbors with his head high and his mouth set in a line.

"I've done stupider things in my time, but I hope not many. From the distance, I just saw you all as a group and I—'' He had to work to make those lips move. "You all, obviously, know Charly."

No one moved to shake hands or greet him, which was about when Charly realized the tension in the yard was as tight as a packed snowball. Whitt was the only one who spoke. "And obviously you do, too. Carson Tanner, isn't it?" At Tanner's nod, Whitt said flatly, "Charly was just kicking us all out. The hour's pretty late to be visiting."

"Yes." Tanner seemed to take her neighbor's wariness for granted. He met Whitt's eyes squarely. "I'm not actually visiting, and I won't be here long or in anyone's way. Charly has something of mine in her barn."

"What do you mean you won't be here long?" Charly abruptly found her voice. She took the last porch step at a stride, cutting through her clutch of neighbors faster than a whip. "Tanner, you're late! Or did I mix up the time? I could have sworn we said seven."

"You never mentioned you knew Tanner, Charly." Lars's voice was low.

"Of course I know him! We're old friends. Half the county stops here for coffee, you know that, and some of you must have met each other sometime. If not— Tanner, this is Whitt Lingstrom...Curt..."

She couldn't make it work, though heaven knows she tried. The introductions were unnecessary. Years back, most of them must have made a passing acquaintance with Tanner, but no one seemed willing to pursue a conversation but her. Undaunted, she kept up a blithe, determined, easy round of patter about Whitt's pretty wife, Curt's newest baby, Lars's ranch and about how Tanner, just like the rest of them, had the Minnesota courtesy to occasionally stop in and see how she was doing. Her message was clear. Tanner was a friend.

She knew the boys heard that message because they all stopped acting like posturing roosters, but no one moved to start their snowmobile engines. The whole time she was talking she couldn't spare a glance at Tanner because she was too busy glaring at her neighbors. *I don't care what you heard. I'm telling you he's all right.*

"I'm freezing my toes off, and your wives are all going to be worried about you if you don't get going. As in ten minutes ago!" she scolded.

"You want some of us to stick around?" Lars's murmur was low, but sound carried in the still night.

"Of course not." Her voice was firm and her color high. It was one thing to distrust a man and another to insult him. She'd never seen her neighbors behave so badly.

Curt mentioned to Tanner, "We only live a couple miles down the road. Fifteen minutes at most from Charly."

By the time they started their snowmobiles, she was so mad at them she was breathing smoke. At the first roar of an engine, though, Tanner's horse nervously reared. She saw him stroke the big horse, talk to him, but even when the sound of engines faded in the distance, his smoke-gray eyes weren't focused on the stallion. They were on her like moonbeams, cool, intense and unfathomable.

"Why did you do that?"

"Do what?" She didn't look at him. His tone was forbidding enough. She looked at his stallion, who was won over with simply a soft word and a stroked nose, unlike his owner.

"Defend me. They were your friends. They were obviously trying to protect you. If you'd given me a chance to get five words in, I would have explained about the owl and put any worries they had to bed. Why on earth did you start that Tanner-you're-late nonsense?"

Maybe because she was doomed to make a fool of herself around him? Charly was all too conscious of having exploded like a firecracker the last time she'd been close to him. In the silent, freezing cold, moon-swept yard, she could still feel the shameless sizzle in her errant heartbeat. Inexcusably she had to remind herself of pride. "Since you brought up the owl, Tanner, I'm glad you're here. He hasn't eaten. He won't eat. I've been worried to death about him. That's why you're here, aren't you? To see George? So I'll take your horse. You just head up to the loft and see if you can do something."

His stallion didn't mind being led, but he shied at the dark barn door. Charly let out the length of reins to reach for the light. Her Belgians all wakened for a look at the newcomer. "I'll rub him down and put him in the far stall. You have any problem with him packing ice in his shoes?"

"No."

His tone was so clipped that she glanced back. In certain light, Tanner looked as tall as a goalpost and just as immovable. His gaze tracked her from straggly ponytail to cold red nose to her father's old jacket, which swallowed her. He was frowning. Not a little frown, but a full-fledged scowl, and she'd suddenly had enough.

"Stash it, Tanner," she said quietly. "Stash the chip on your shoulder and stash the frown. Neither is worth mincemeat with me, and neither is necessary."

"*Now* what are you talking about?"

"I'm talking about you being pretty good at making people afraid of you. Afraid. Intimidated. Nervous. Heaven knows you had the boys pawing the yard out there like frisky ponies." She led his stallion to a tie stall. "Actually, the look of those nuts had to be one of the funniest things I've ever seen."

"Funny? People don't much trust me in the area. Haven't you noticed? Hasn't it occurred to you that they might have reason? And I rode in with a gun drawn—"

"From the distance of the north woods, you saw a lone woman surrounded by four men," she said softly. "That's what happened, wasn't it?"

"I came to make sure the owl wasn't giving you trouble. That's all," he said harshly.

"Fine. Whatever you do, don't take credit for trying to do a nice thing, Tanner. You'd obviously climb a wall if someone dared to offer you a thank-you." She used a handful of straw to dry off his horse. "And the idea of the boys protecting me is pure horseradish. I grew up with every one of those turkeys. They know me as well as peanut butter and jelly. For that matter, there isn't one of them that hasn't seen me naked."

Silence followed, as potent as the shock of a lightning bolt. The word *naked* had done it. By the time she crossed to the other side of his stallion, she had a good glimpse of the cold censure in his eyes. He couldn't possibly know how honored she was by that censure, but that didn't stop her humorous chuckle.

"Come on, Tanner. Are you blind? All you have to do is look at me to know that I didn't mean naked *that* way. We all used to skinny-dip in the creek as kids. I've fished with Howe and Lars, hunted and camped with Whitt, studied finals with Curt."

She didn't add that the only time the "boys" had forgotten her was at prom time. Charly was just one of the guys. It had never occurred to any of them to ask her out, just as it would never occur to their wives to worry about the men occasionally spending the long winter hours at Charly's place. What was the harm? Charly was just Charly.

Some days that hurt so much it felt like a knife in her chest.

And it hurt now, but that was exactly why she'd made the comment about "naked." Pride had a stepladder of levels. At one level, it was painful to goad him into looking at her—*really* looking at her—in order to remind him that a promiscuous life-style was hardly likely for a woman with her looks. But that level of pride could be sacrificed. To have Tanner know she was attracted to him, that she'd worried about him as a woman worries about a man...no. How could she end up anything but looking foolish if he knew how she really felt?

"Nobody protects me, Tanner, because I can protect myself," she continued blithely. "And it's about time you figured out that you don't need to get defensive around me, either. Some women may bother you, but I'd be hard-pressed to believe I was one of them. I grew up with men all my life and never threatened one of them yet."

She stroked his stallion one last time and then eased out of the tie stall, conscious of Tanner's silence. Too conscious. "You know where the first-aid supplies are for George. I'll be in the house brewing a fresh pot of coffee. If you want some, fine. If you don't, don't. But if you come in the house, you make sure you leave that chip on the back porch."

She left without giving him a chance to answer. She hadn't expected an answer. He'd come for the owl, not for her, and as he'd soon find out, George was more than a handful.

If he came in after that, well, she'd just have to see. But as she opened her back door, the image of Tanner galloping through the night with his cocked rifle refused to leave her. There was only one conclusion she could reach. He'd thought she was in trouble.

After seeing the way her neighbors treated him, Charly thought that he was in a lot of trouble. Tanner hadn't reached out to any of them, but there'd been an imperceptible moment when he'd loosened his right hand from the reins of his horse—the one he'd have used to shake hands with, if the gesture had been offered.

She hung up her jacket and wandered into the kitchen to make coffee. At that precise moment her pride didn't seem so important. Tanner was alone. Painfully alone. A condition no one could understand as well as Charly.

Four

I can see how she's been treating you, George. No wonder you haven't been behaving. Fresh bedding every day, prime mouse steak, lights left on for you. I could have guessed she'd spoil you rotten."

As soon as the wing was rebandaged and a stronger sling secured, Tanner removed the owl's blindfold and switched off Charly's battery lantern. The upper story of the barn promptly went blank as ink.

Waiting, Tanner folded himself in the corner, bringing up one knee for an elbow rest. "Did you hear her talking downstairs? The lady has a real problem. I'm telling you, if a robber walked in her house, she'd offer him the silver and aim her gun at the posse."

In the darkness, sounds intensified. He heard the instant the bird's claws shifted on the perch.

"You know when she got to me?" Tanner irritably plucked off his gloves. "All that business about how she's never threatened a man yet. She wasn't talking about a physical threat, George, she was talking about sex. I know she didn't say the word, but that's what she meant. Like it never once occurred to her that a man could be attracted... I suppose you think I'm reading a lot into what she said downstairs."

George sidestepped all the way to his food dish, only to discover the Stetson and red bandanna covering the tray. Tanner heard the whoosh when his hat flew to the floor. The bandanna dropped soundlessly on his knee.

"Maybe I am," Tanner continued softly. "Hell, I don't know her. I do know what I thought when I saw her from the woods, surrounded by all those men. We both know the lady lacks a certain self-protective instinct, George. We're talking about a woman who's warm and sassy and real—and who lets any riffraff in her back door. How was I supposed to know those guys were her friends?"

Tanner heard the bird tear into the dead mouse and winced. George was not a delicate eater. "Sure, she's safe as a church with me. I'm not about to drag a woman into my life-style, but that's the reason she's safe, George. Not because I think she's plain or un-attractive or some other fool nonsense." He paused. "Still hungry, are you?"

He lurched to his feet and switched on the lantern. Charly had set ample traps. He dropped another mouse in the empty dish, covered it meticulously with his bandanna and hat again, then flicked off the lantern. The whole time George stared at the wall, proudly indifferent, bored enough to blink. Until the light was off.

"There's only one reason I *might* amble over for coffee in her kitchen, George. You know she has borderland, don't you? Isolated as hell. And I told you we're having a quiet little problem with cocaine sneaking across the river. She'd never even hear a few snowmobiles on her back forty, and we both know she's inclined to take strangers at face value. I'm not doubting she could handle a horse, a renegade wolf. It's just men where she has this little problem. And I'll be damned if I can get the picture out of my head of her skinny-dipping with all those—"

Abruptly he groped for his well-pecked hat, dropped it on his head and rose to his feet. "I'll be back, George," he whispered. "But no more giving her a hard time. You hear me?"

Downstairs he checked on his horse, doused the barn lights and headed for Charly's house.

He only rapped once on the door, and when she didn't immediately answer, he found himself freezing up, his muscles taut and his pulse climbing. How do you have a tactful little talk with a capable adult woman about being careful about men?

She wasn't his business and he didn't belong here.

He'd changed his mind and taken three strides back toward the barn when he heard the twist of the doorknob. "Tanner? You have in mind freezing or coming in?"

His stomach had the going-down-the-elevator feeling that he'd experienced when he'd been caught redhanded as a kid. Fibbing to himself went against his grain. He knew darn well that reasons for wanting to see her had little to do with a lecture on safety. "I only wanted to tell you that the owl was okay. And eating. I have to get going."

"I know. It's late, also colder than a brass ice cube. You really want to head back out without a chance to warm up for a few minutes?"

He came in clutching his hat, aware that his hair was unbrushed and that his face looked whisker rough. He felt edgy and stiff because he could feel a pull inside him like the tug of a rope. Never mind what was right, the warmth of her house and her red-and-white-checked kitchen soothed him like salve on a burn. There was a distinctly sassy fire in her eyes when she reached up to flick something invisible from his jacket's lapels.

"You were going to leave those chips on your shoulders outside, remember?" she said cheerfully. "Now, you want coffee or brandy? And are you hungry?"

"Neither and no. Look, I just wanted to tell you..." He remembered the last time she'd touched him and figured that she made a point of touching him this time to show off how natural and no-nonsense-comfortable a woman she was to be around. Only that wasn't what he saw in her eyes, and he suddenly couldn't remember what he wanted to tell her.

"Yes, about the owl," she said smoothly. "Come on through when you have your gear off." She was gone.

He shed his coat and boots and in stockinged feet tracked her as far as her kitchen doorway, then stopped. Her living room had been in darkness the last time he'd seen it. It wasn't now.

Flames shot up the corner fireplace, which was soot-blackened old, well loved and well used. The walls were a muted French blue. Family photographs took up half the bookshelves. From rugs to furniture, nothing was fancy, but he could smell flowers, hot brandy, fragrance, wood smoke. The smells of a home.

His place still had all his mother's trappings. It still looked like a home, but it didn't *smell* like one. He hadn't been in a home since he could remember. Like the tease of a candy for a diabetic, he felt himself drawn, tempted, pulled to what he shouldn't want and couldn't have.

"Come in and put your feet up, Tanner. My furniture's used to it, and you look whipped."

She'd settled in an overstuffed chair. Her legs were curled under her, making it more than clear that she wasn't treating him with any special deference. A pair of oversize glasses perched on her nose, and she was holding some strange rectangle thing on her lap—it looked like a wooden picture frame with a dozen white satin spools of thread hanging from it. Her fingers flew, flipping those spools, pausing only long enough to motion at the wooden tray on the coffee table.

"They're both hot—one's coffee and the other's a rose-marigold brandy. Don't keep me in suspense forever. How did you get our ornery devil to eat?"

He couldn't stop watching her fingers flip the white satin spools. "I covered his dish, which didn't give him much of a challenge, but some. George has never had food in his life come easy, so I guessed it upset him. And I turned out the lights. You'd been leaving the lantern on for him, Charly, which was sweet, but owls aren't sweet. Owls are scavenging beg-your-pardon bastards who associate the darkness with eating time—'' He added abruptly, ''What did you say the brandy was?''

She tipped him a grin. ''Rose-marigold—an old vice. Not the drinking of it, the making of it. Be brave. Give it a try.''

He poured, then sipped. Then sipped again. There was the scent of flowers but not the taste. The taste was smooth, potent and dangerous. Almost as dangerous as her firelight and the warmth of her old-fashioned room. He stayed standing. ''Your brandy's good.''

''Don't look so shocked,'' she said dryly.

Shock wasn't his problem. Hunger was. Prowling about the room, he touched the fringe on a silk lamp shade, studied her family photographs, touched a lace-edged pillow.

His restlessness didn't seem to bother her. She kept up a steady stream of conversation about her Belgians. ''Your family used to raise horses, didn't they, Tanner? I think I love the winters most, just because the summers are so crazy around here. The young foals are part of that, and in season I end up housing as many as twenty mares in the back barn. Added to that, Blitz brings in the best money if I take him on the road. He's stood for fillies as far away as northern New York.''

Tanner listened, but less to what she said than to her soothing low voice. She could talk a cat down from a tree with that voice, calm a child's nightmares, tame the edginess right out of a man if he wasn't careful. Tanner was always careful, but his own silence was starting to nag at him. He couldn't remember the last time he'd tried to talk to a woman. Just talk. Conversation. Maybe he didn't know how anymore. "Do you mind if I ask you what you're doing?"

"Making lace." Her green eyes peered at him over the rim of her glasses with just a trace of wariness.

"Lace?" he repeated.

"I may train and breed horses, Tanner, but in the winter I make lace. Of course, you tell anyone I make lace and please don't doubt that I have the strength to break your bones." She set aside the wooden frame and unfolded herself from the chair. "Fill up your glass—good heavens, you don't expect me to wait on you, do you? Since you obviously can't settle down, I'll give you a treat and show you my Ophrys."

He had no idea what an "Ophrys" was, but the image of her breaking his bones had a grin on his lips. Charly's humor was always unexpected and almost as sneaky as her brandy.

She switched on a light past a tall oak grandfather clock, then opened a curtain that he thought covered a window and instead covered a door.

When he stepped inside, he stepped from winter to spring. The little room was more atrium than greenhouse, but it was still big enough for the flush of light warm air and scents and sights to startle him. For a lady who kept her barn pin neat and bluntly talked stud fees, this room was a feminine explosion of colors and wildness. Nothing was neat, nothing kept orderly. Everywhere were her roses, her marigolds and pots on pots of vibrant, strangely shaped flowers in passionate reds and fuchsias and deep clear blues.

"Orchids, Tanner. Another vice of mine, and as well kept a secret as my lace. Don't ask me how I keep this up in the summer. I knew when I started it that they were an insane hobby to have. Mostly I have cattleyas, but there are a few rare ones, a few Ophrys, a few trigenerics. There's no sexier plant on earth than an orchid. About fifteen hundred years ago, people used to eat the tubers for their aphrodisiac quality, which, of course, is nonsense. However..."

He sipped at her brandy and listened, bemused, as she gave him a thorough and graphic lecture on sex. The sex life of her orchids.

"The most noticeable part of any orchid is the lip, properly called the labellum. That lip's a landing strip for an insect to land on, because orchids need pollinators. And because orchids need pollinators, the flower has developed some extremely sexy and sultry methods of wooing her pollinators...."

She was wearing a yellow blouse over jeans. It was just a plain yellow blouse, but when she moved her hands around, its V neck revealed a hint of pale blue silk. Hardly de rigueur underwear for a rancher. Tanner tried, hard, to keep thinking of her as a rancher.

"This one has a bucket-shaped lip. You see? The orchid draws the insect to that lip with a scent, then the lip closes up on the bug for, say, maybe as long as an hour and a half. By the time she releases the bug, it's drugged high as a kite and very, very happy. So's the orchid, because she's managed to get herself pollinated. I'm not boring you, am I, Tanner?"

"No."

"Are you sure?"

"I am very sure."

"With the Ophrys, we have another pollination concept that the scientists delicately call pseudocopulation."

"Tell me, Charly."

She did. His friends had never been this explicit when they'd all gone behind a barn when he was nine. Again he found himself smiling, but not as easily as before. Wisps of hair kept sneaking on her cheek; she avoided his eyes and he could hardly miss the gentle careful point she was making. The lady talked about sex with a botanist's clinical interest, something like a woman who yawned after a man made a pass. The message was clear to him. *Just in case you were still worried, Tanner, the little spinster isn't going to jump your bones.*

When she switched out the light, he closed the door to her greenhouse, then stopped there.

"What's wrong?"

"Nothing. It's just...I'm just not sure why you did this. Your brandy. Your lace. Your orchids. You the same as said they were secrets, so why show me?"

She didn't answer for a minute, because she left the room. When she came back she was carrying his jacket and scarf and hat, which she handed him one at a time. "You keep secrets, Tanner. I keep mine. Sometime, maybe, you're going to need someone to talk to. I just made the first move, that's all. Now, get out of here. It's late."

She bossed like a shrew, even when he had his boots on and was at the back door. She played the role of mother/sister/friend well. In fact, she had the role down to a science. "You'll be back to check on your owl. If I'm not here, just let yourself in the back door and help yourself to coffee. Everyone knows I keep the door unlocked. Now give us a kiss and be on your way.''

She reached up to buss his cheek, a grandmother's peck, sexless and simple and, he guessed, yet another way she'd chosen to show him who she was. She was not a woman who fired with passion in the darkness of a barn with a stranger, but Charly. Just Charly. A woman that a man could count on for a dinner or a listening ear, a place to relax or a mug of hot black coffee. But nothing more.

When he reached for her, he couldn't have said why he acted the way he did. Maybe it was the orchids or the lace. Maybe Charly was too damn young to kiss like a maiden aunt, and maybe he was mad at her because she said she never locked her door. He told himself that anger was the cause. Only anger had never felt quite like this. He traced the line of her cheek with a tenderness alien to him, a gentleness not in character, and then she looked at him with those jade-green eyes.

He took her mouth. The last time he'd kissed her had been to scare her. This was something far less reasonable. He rubbed his lips over hers, silk on silk, something soft, just for her, something nice. The pulse in her throat tightened under his thumb; she arched her throat and made a soft wild sound. A haunted sound, like a trapped animal.

He was the one who felt trapped. When his tongue swirled on hers, he tasted sweetness, danger, darkness. He told himself to stop. Nothing about this was right. He had no business anywhere near her; she had no business kissing him back. But he couldn't seem to force himself away from her taste. From her warmth. From her willingness. Dammit, slap me, Charly, he silently begged.

She gulped in air when his mouth left hers, but she didn't move. His whiskered jaw had to bruise her soft face when he rubbed against her hair, her temples, her jawline. She didn't seem to care. Her hands sneaked up his arms until they wrapped around his neck. Her fingertips were cold on his neck, a measure of her nervousness. Her lips were trembling and her eyes had a bewildered burn. She didn't seem all that sure of what she was doing. He was. *Honey, I'd give you a loaded gun, but you'd still have to have the good sense to aim it at me.*

It had been so long since he'd felt drawn into a woman's silken net, since he'd felt the allure of passion, smelled the fragrance and touched the texture of a woman's skin. He'd slept with a rifle too many cold nights, a thousand cold nights, and Charly... Charly was the temptation of fire. He had his jacket on. She had her clothes on. But when he finished another string of hungry kisses she was sandwiched between a hard wall and him and he couldn't have let her go for all the gold in the world.

He slid his hands down her spine, feeling her cotton blouse slip-slide over a silky undergarment. Beneath the fabric, he could feel her supple skin heat and yield. He wanted to feel her bare, and he knew she wanted touching. She wanted it so much she was trembling, and wildly, awkwardly, she reached for his mouth again. She bumped his nose instead. He found himself smiling; he kissed her a smile and then he kissed her in a different way, carefully, thoroughly teaching her the geography of a kiss because she didn't seem to know how to make lips and tongues and noses fit. It was all so easy. It was all so nice. And he was going out of his mind.

Tentatively, shyly, as if not at all sure of his reaction or approval, Charly slid her hands down his jacketed spine to his hips. His reaction damn near busted the zipper on his jeans, and as far as approval, his temperature rose to three hundred and ten. Needs trampled through him. He fought them back.

"Put your hands back up on my shoulders, honey. Now."

"I—"

"Now!" He inhaled a lungful of air. "Hell and damnation. What are you *doing*, woman?"

What she seemed to be doing was smiling. The woman didn't have a lick of sense. His fiercest scowl could have intimidated a grizzly, and she just stood there with her blouse half undone and that smile and those woman's green eyes looking protective. Protective! "Don't you know what you were inviting?" he snapped at her.

"You were never going to let anything go that far." Her whisper was clear, gentle. "I trust you."

"Trust no one. No one, Charly, not in this life and least of all me." He jammed the hat on his head, breathing hard and harshly, and when he hurled open the door he made the hinges rattle. "Lock your damned door and keep it locked."

"Yes, Tanner."

"You keep it locked all the time when you're alone in this house."

"Yes, Tanner."

He slammed down her porch steps two at a time, knowing damn well she wasn't going to. The cold air hit his face like a punch and the brandy had his stomach rolling. Or she did. *Something* did. He was riled up enough to take on a cougar, his brain was fuzzy, and he told himself in no uncertain terms that he had to leave her alone.

He was back two days later, and two days after that. Charly never actually saw him, but each time she was somehow awakened at midnight. Her head had been groggy from sleep, yet she'd found herself climbing out of bed and pulling on her old blue robe and padding barefoot to her kitchen window, where she'd seen the faint flicker of lantern light reflecting from the upper story of her barn.

Tonight was Sunday. He'd skipped three days this time from his last visit. Sipping a glass of water in her dark kitchen, Charly yet again found her eyes riveted to the lighted barn window, her bare feet freezing and the clock ticking at an abominable 12:07 a.m.

Something was wrong tonight. She could feel it. *Never mind. You're not going out there, Charly.*

She sipped more water, well aware that the hours Tanner chose to visit made it obvious that he had come to caretake his owl, not to see her. That he didn't simply take the owl told her something else. He couldn't care for George himself, but was it because of work hours or traveling or an undependable schedule? The "whys" didn't really matter. He obviously would have if he could have. He cared enough about the bird to keep coming miles out of his way, to maintain incredibly odd hours, to risk exposure on a subzero night to see him.

She understood why he didn't want to see her. Hell's bells, she'd come on to him like a mare in heat both times they had been alone together. What would a hero of a handsome devil like him want with plain, staid old Charly? She'd embarrassed him twice now, and twice her pride had taken the licking.

So it's very simple. You're not going out there, Charly.

She sipped more water. Actually, she gulped the last from the glass. All her life she'd have chosen to eat straw, suffer the flu or break a leg rather than make a fool of herself with a man. She'd done that only once before Tanner. It wasn't an occasion she was likely to forget.

It had been the night of her twenty-fifth birthday. Soul-searching came naturally with landmark birthdays, and so she had been doing just that. After several daiquiris, a drink she'd never had before and certainly never since, she'd come to several conclusions. She was reasonably proud of what she was doing with her life; there were worse things than being single; and the unattached men running around her neck of the woods simply weren't looking at Charly— or likely to.

Those three conclusions didn't cause her any trouble; it was the fourth one. Maybe she didn't mind being single, but there was no way on this earth she was willing to die a virgin.

She'd picked a stranger. Knowing it was wrong. Knowing he didn't care a hoot and knowing the only thing in his head was giving the unattractive little spinster a whirl.

Even good people sometimes did stupid things. For Charly, that was definitely the highlight. Intellectually she hadn't expected anything from the encounter, but she'd gone into it with a headful of romantic illusions and wistful needs and a girl's dreams. One humiliating night had readily cured those.

No question that she'd gotten what she'd asked for, but since then she had been meticulously *not* foolish. No man was coming that close to damaging her pride again. That resolution had been easy to make and easy to keep. Until Tanner.

She poured herself another glass of water, still staring at the lighted barn window. *Forget it, Charly. You're not going out there.*

There would be no problem at all if she could just quit worrying about him. For reasons she couldn't fathom he had no one. That night in the yard, she knew he could have turned around her neighbors' wariness with a dozen friendly words. He hadn't spoken them, hadn't tried. And a man who roamed around at midnight to take care of an owl wasn't logical. Or sane. Or even healthy.

She gulped more water. He rejected the simplest offers of kindness and warmth, yet like a starved wolf prowling the woods' edge, the lonesomeness was raw on his face. What *did* he do with his time? If he'd really been thrown out of Customs for theft or contraband, wouldn't he have been in jail? What could he ever have done that was so awful that he'd locked himself in such a lonely life-style?

He could have killed people, Charly, and you're not going out there.

She slammed her glass on the counter, made a quick trip to the bathroom—that *had* been her third glass of water—and came out through the back hall reaching for her jacket. Cursing, she pushed her bare feet in boots and tromped outside.

When her robe's hem dipped in the night's six inches of fresh snow, she muttered again. The temperature hovered around ten below. It was now past one. Beneath the jacket, her ragtag robe was as old as the hills; her unbrushed hair was streaming down her back and she had to look ridiculous.

You got that right, Charly. What's more, you still have time to turn around and go right back inside the house where you belong. Why can't you leave him alone? He's going to think you're chasing him. He's going to think the lady's desperate to get laid. Dammit, where's your pride?

She seemed to have left it back at the house. As she strode through the dark first story of her barn, her stomach was clenched in a fist of anxiety and her heart pounded dread...or maybe shame. Still, she flew past her Belgians without a pet or a carrot or even a whisper.

Something was wrong. She heard no sound coming from above. If the lighted lantern hadn't been casting shadows, she would have doubted anyone was there. Tanner's horse wasn't stabled below.

She tiptoed up the steps, not an easy accomplishment in boots, until she climbed halfway up. Then she stopped dead for the space of ten seconds, before rushing hell-bent for leather the rest of the way.

"Tanner, damn you! What have you done?"

He was there, all right. Slumped against the cage door with his head leaning back and his eyes closed. One eye was swollen shut. There was a huge gash on his cheek, and his color was ash gray. As far as she could tell, he was unconscious.

Five

Tanner had never intended to fall asleep, never knew he had. Exhaustion had snuck up on him like a poison. When he first heard the voice, he thought he was still in the woods with a man reaching for him from behind. Instincts functioned stronger than conscious thought. He automatically reached for his rifle.

By the time he recognized Charly, she'd already kicked his gun out of reach and was all over him. His head had a lot in common with a well pit; the blackness refused to leave. All he had was a disorienting view of swinging blond hair, a threadbare blue robe, furious jade-green eyes and cool gentle fingertips on his cheek.

Her voice wasn't so gentle. Tanner might not be able to make himself snap to, but she pelted questions at him so fast that he responded blindly. "That's quite a door you ran into, Tanner. I can see the face, but what's wrong with your side?''

"Nothing."

"We'll see. Now are you dizzy? Nauseous?"

"No."

"You are, too. And I know you were hit on the head because I can see the blood. Hard enough to worry about concussion?"

"Get out of here, Charly."

There were times when he wanted nothing more in life than to crush his face against a woman's breasts. Hers, however, were covered by the scraggly robe and zippered jacket—the zipper darn near poked him in the eye—and her fingers were all over his scalp. "I don't feel any goose eggs, but let's see how you do standing up."

He didn't want to stand up. He wanted to bite someone, preferably her, particularly when he made an outstanding effort at lurching to his feet and found himself dizzy as a drunk.

"I'm *fine*. How did you even know I was here? And what were you doing out in the barn this late?" Descending the stairs made his head clang. He'd counted on that stopping when they reached the main floor. They had; it hadn't.

"What I'm doing is obvious. I'm carting a stupid man off to bed."

"I'm not going into your house."

She already had an arm clutched tight around his waist. Now she swung that arm full length and delivered it level to his backside. The contact stung. She had a heck of a swing. "Now behave!"

For a moment he was totally silent. He smelled the horses and the leather and knew where he was. But it hurt to focus: it hurt to breathe, and his body felt as if someone had run over it with a Mack truck. At high speed.

Time refused to catch up for him. He kept seeing the fist aiming at him, the dead black eyes and the silence of a bleak isolated night that he'd faced before. Either you won or you died. He'd been there a thousand times. The taste of violence was still with him, the smell of contact with the lowest form of life, the rage at the prices he paid to do what he did.

"What are you smiling at, Tanner?"

The words slipped out. "At you. Spanking me."

They were in her yard by then, the wind battering him and his lungs sucking in the cold. Charly chose that idiotic moment to chuckle. "First time I've seen anything take the starch out of you, which I will certainly remember for another time. Are you going to tell me about the steamroller you ran into?"

"No."

"And that's no surprise." She released him in order to climb the porch steps and push open her back door. "Don't try arguing with me about coming in."

He grappled for balance. "I could use coffee." He didn't like to admit to need or weakness, but his truck was parked a half mile down the road. Sooner or later his body would start behaving. It had to, but at the moment a half-mile walk sounded as appealing as a timed lap across the Pacific.

"You're not getting any coffee. You're getting some ice for that eye, some aspirin, someone to pull off your boots for you and a bed. No coffee." She didn't look so stubborn and contrary; the wind was tangling her long hair in silken ropes. Her skin was pale. Her gaze swept his face, softly, possessively, and her voice was a whisper. "Where did you get the idea it was so wrong to need someone, Tanner?"

But needing people was wrong for him. His choices had been made a long time ago by a rigid taskmaster of a conscience. That conscience had never failed him before.

Over the past ten days he'd told himself he was only returning for George. The owl was his problem, his responsibility. Tanner had yet to find a bandage that George couldn't get at, and rebandaging the bad-tempered devil involved direct exposure to one beak and eight lethally sharp claws. If Tanner hadn't returned, that problem would have been left for Charly.

He'd told himself over and over that he'd only come back for the owl, but at the moment his head was soup and her yard light a dizzy, dizzy yellow. Honesty battered him as ruthlessly as the wind.

Tonight he'd known himself in no shape to caretake George. He'd known himself in no shape to be anywhere but his own house and his own bed, and he'd still come. He'd wanted her to find him. He wanted her to care. He wanted her to sneak those feminine little looks at him and he wanted to yell at her about locking her door and he wanted her to tell him all about the sex life of her orchids and he wanted . . .

He *wanted* to be able to think, but her porch posts suddenly blurred and doubled. Faster than a heartbeat, she tucked herself under his armpit and grabbed for him. "That's it, Tanner. You just ran out of choices. We're doing this my way."

It seemed that they were. His focus clicked from color to black and white like a TV screen going haywire; either the world was moving or he was. She never let him go until they'd reached the long hall to a bedroom. Still wearing his jacket, he found himself sitting on a bed and staring at her backside. She seemed to have one of his boots between her legs and she was telling him to use her fanny for a foot brace.

He couldn't do that. Even with an eye swollen shut and a hammering headache, he knew his boots were crusted with mud and ice. "Come on, Tanner," she goaded him. "You're not dealing with a pink-and-white Barbie Doll. You're dealing with me. I can't get your boots off without a little help. Give us a push."

Later, he never remembered giving the "royal we" a push. What energy he had seemed to spin in vague focus around the room. It may have lacked frills and baubles, but no one else would have paired mauve with a pale celery green but a woman. The lights were soft and the textures muted and sensual.

He said he wanted his gun. Charly—good Lord, the woman had a man's vocabulary when she was irritated—accused him of using his gun the way a kid used a security blanket. She informed him she'd let him know when he needed his rifle and that wasn't now.

The next thing he knew there was an ice bag pressed on his eye. She was peeling off his jacket as if she were undressing a child. Her robe parted when she was kneeling over him and caused the first shock of elemental sanity he'd had in hours.

Charly slept naked. She didn't have a stitch on under the robe.

"I assume we're dealing with a massive headache. I'll get some water and aspirin. For heaven's sake, stay there. I don't want to come in and have to pick you up off the floor."

She brought the aspirin but didn't give him a chance to take it. She was applying a cool washcloth to the cut on his lip and he seemed to be lying down, which was not an issue of illness but slipperiness. Her comforter was as slick as a slide. To keep his eyes off the gaping throat of her robe, he forced his gaze to wander. An ounce of powder-pink lace was crumpled on a dresser, the matching panties were on the mauve carpet. His gaze jumped back to her.

"This isn't your spare room."

"Would you not talk? I can't clean you up when you're fidgeting."

He was *not* fidgeting. He'd never fidgeted in his life. When she'd finally cleaned and bandaged to her satisfaction, he barely had the chance to swallow the aspirin before she was tugging at his jeans. "I think we've finally found a definitely human flaw, Tanner. You must have a strong streak of masculine vanity if you're wearing jeans this tight. Whoops! Sorry."

He considered himself lucky she left him his underwear, because she took his jeans. She took his shirt. She took the glass of water and pushed him under the comforter and turned out the light. It wasn't that she moved fast but she did move efficiently, like a woman who'd decided what to do and was simply doing it. The last thing she evidently decided was that he needed sleep—now, with no talk and no arguments.

When it came down to it, she never gave him a chance to argue before she closed the door behind her and left him.

Rather bewilderingly fast, he found himself totally alone. He let the ice pack slip to the floor, closed his eyes, and felt the first wave of exhaustion seep through him.

He didn't have to fight it now, and he didn't. He fought the swamping hint of roses instead, the sheets so soft they didn't belong near a man's skin, the swallowing thick comforter that had her scent, her warmth...she normally slept in this bed naked, did she? And with her hair loose, with her cheek cuddled into this pillow, with her full white breasts draped between these sheets.

He couldn't be farther from knives and fists, from woods as black as the eyes of his prey, from the tastes of risk and danger.

Yet he couldn't be emotionally farther from Charly than if he lived in another country. Most often he could avoid a violent confrontation, but not always. And the isolation of his job was the greater drawback. How could he ask a woman to share that?

But in those few brief moments before sleep took him, he banished his honor and his conscience and allowed the seep of need, desire, want. A man could pretend anything in the dark.

A man could pretend, for example, that Charly was right here and that he was far too weak to fight her uninhibited sensual assault. She was bare as a nymph and wantonly making love to him. He tried to slow her down by winding her long hair around her breasts and whispering to her—not about right and wrong, not about what could and couldn't be, but whispers about how pretty her breasts were, how he loved her wild mouth and her long, long legs. She wasn't interested in sweet talk; she took him inside her. Hard and deep. She rode him like an unbroken stallion, taking *him* instead of the other way around, and that with a whore's lusty freedom and a virgin's willful, sweet, precious explosion of innocence. He murmured extremely honorable words about protecting her virtue, but what could he do? She wasn't listening so it wasn't *his* fault. *Lord,* she wanted him. The woman was just plain out of her mind with wanting him, and . . .

Tanner, why don't we put this fairy tale to bed before you fall flat on your face en route to a cold shower?

He thought that if she had any sense at all she'd have shot him when she had the gun. And then he slept.

Getting Blitzen in a horse trailer was like stuffing a mouse into a trap. The spirit of enthusiasm was lacking. When a 2200-pound horse didn't want to do something, he generally got the idea that he didn't have to.

"If I'd just had you as a colt, you'd have known who was boss," Charly muttered. With one hand on the reins, she delivered a sharp slap to the horse's flank. "Now move!"

Blitz swished his sassy cropped tail, and behind her, Wes Small chuckled. "Get the cat," the wizened old vet advised.

"That's ridiculous!" But after two more aborted tries, Charly flipped Wes the reins and stalked for the barn and Blitzen's stall. In the far corner a mangy cat was curled in the straw, washing her face. Charly scooped her up and moments later pelted up the trailer ramp, ignoring Wes's gusty laughter. Blitzen, now meek as a lamb, climbed in the trailer with no coaxing or encouragement from anyone.

"Will the cat ride? Because otherwise I'll be stuck with the same problem at the other end."

"Oh, she'll ride," Charly said dryly. "She's ridden all over the country with him now. Those fools are so inseparable it's embarrassing. It's just I had in mind drumming up a little business out of this horse show. You know, showing off his never-defeated champion ribbons, his character, his style, his bloodlines. Now he's going to arrive there looking like a big baby."

Again Wes chuckled, helping her remove the ramp and close up the trailer. "Come on, Charly. He won't be the first horse to get attached to a small critter."

"I know that, but he could have had the good taste to pick a Persian or a Siamese or a cat with class. Scrubbs won't even mouse!" Before Wes could climb in the pickup, she hurled her arms around him in a massive hug, delivered in between a dozen instructions. "You'll watch his feed? He'll cramp up if he gets too many oats. And he gets nervous when he first sees a crowd—"

"Honey, I've been his vet for four years. Don't you think I know him?"

"I should go." Charly ran a hand through her hair. "If it was Prancer, I know he'd behave for you. But Blitz is such a handful."

Wes snorted. "In case you need reminding, I've been handling horses since you were in diapers."

"I know, I know, but I still feel guilty."

"That's just because you think you have to do everything yourself. I've told you before, you don't take near enough advantage of me. I got time coming out of my ears with this semiretired business, and I love a horse show." Wes climbed in the driver's seat of the pickup. "As I also told you before, young lady, you need full-time help around here."

This was old news. "I have full-time help in the spring, and Lars is always willing to hire on for a day or two if I have to be gone," she reminded him. "I wouldn't have had to ask you for help if he didn't just come down with the flu."

"I'm not interested in Lars's flu." Once inside the truck, Wes snapped the seat belt and cranked down the window. "I'm interested in you realizing that you're running a fine edge between what one person can handle and what one person can't."

"You want me to finish out the lecture?" Charly murmured peaceably. "I know the rest by heart."

Wes stiffened his jaw. "A big strong man better take you on before you're *all* starch and sass. I'd do it myself if I were forty years younger."

Charly laughed, and Wes escaped before she managed to give him another four hundred instructions. She watched the truck and trailer leave the yard and then glanced at her watch. The late hour appalled her. Wes had arrived in the middle of morning chores. She'd needed him to take a look at her pregnant mares and then there was getting Blitzen off. One way or another, she hadn't made it back to the house in four hours.

She peeled off her gloves as she crossed the sun-glazed snow. All morning she'd run on bursts of crazy energy. Even as she shed her winter gear in the back hall, she wasn't sure if her misbehaving heartbeat was due more to anticipation or anxiety. Was he finally awake and up? And what was she going to do with him if he was?

Tanner couldn't know how many hours she'd checked on him in the night. Dead asleep, he proved wonderfully manageable, but no man got battered like that from a simple scuffle in a barroom. Once she really got a look at the bruises, she couldn't imagine how he was still standing. Except that Tanner, like his owl, was stubborn enough to keep fighting when any intelligent creature would be happily sacked out in a coma.

Taking him in had never been a choice. Charly's pride hadn't disappeared, nor the sexual voltage that happened whenever she was near him. Like the verse in the Bible about seasons, though, there was a time for those things. Last night wasn't it. Last night she'd simply reacted to need—one human being to another.

Wrapping her arms under her chest, she hurried toward the kitchen and abruptly stopped. Tanner was up. He had to be, because the bubbling pot of savory stew on the stove hadn't been started by her. She lifted the lid and sniffed, bemused and then startled when she saw her morning dishes were done.

She paused again in the living room. Her fireplace was swept free of ashes and a fresh fire laid but not lit. Inside her bedroom, the bed was made and the sheets tucked army style. She hadn't made a bed beyond throwing a comforter on it in years.

FIRST-CLASS ROMANCE

Mail This Heart TODAY!

And We'll Deliver:

**4 FREE BOOKS
A FREE DIGITAL
CLOCK/CALENDAR
PLUS A SURPRISE
MYSTERY BONUS
TO YOUR DOOR!**

See Inside For More Details

SILHOUETTE® DELIVERS FIRST-CLASS ROMANCE— DIRECT TO YOUR DOOR

Mail the Heart sticker on the postpaid order card today and you'll receive:

—4 new Silhouette Desire® novels—FREE
—a lovely lucite digital clock/calendar—FREE
—and a surprise mystery bonus—FREE

But that's not all. You'll also get:

Money-Saving Home Delivery

When you subscribe to Silhouette Desire®, the excitement, romance and faraway adventures of these novels can be yours for previewing in the convenience of your own home. Every month we'll deliver 6 new books right to your door. If you decide to keep them, they'll be yours for only $2.24* each—that's 26 cents below the cover price, and there is *no* extra charge for postage and handling! There is no obligation to buy— you can cancel at any time simply by writing "cancel" on your statement or by returning a shipment of books to us at our cost.

Free Monthly Newsletter

It's the indispensable insider's look at our most popular writers and their upcoming novels. Now you can have a behind-the-scenes look at the fascinating world of Silhouette! It's an added bonus you'll look forward to every month!

Special Extras—FREE

Because our home subscribers are our most valued readers, we'll be sending you additional free gifts from time to time in your monthly book shipments as a token of our appreciation.

OPEN YOUR MAILBOX TO A WORLD OF LOVE AND ROMANCE EACH MONTH. JUST COMPLETE, DETACH AND MAIL YOUR FREE-OFFER CARD TODAY!

*Terms and prices subject to change without notice.

Remember! To receive your free books, digital clock/calendar and mystery gift, return the postpaid card below. But don't delay!

DETACH AND MAIL CARD TODAY.

If offer card has been removed, write to:
Silhouette Books, 901 Fuhrmann Blvd., P.O. Box 1867, Buffalo, NY 14269-1867

MAIL THE POSTPAID CARD TODAY!

BUSINESS REPLY CARD

First Class   Permit No. 717   Buffalo, NY

Postage will be paid by addressee

Silhouette Books®
901 Fuhrmann Blvd.
P.O. Box 1867
Buffalo, NY 14240-9952

NO POSTAGE
NECESSARY
IF MAILED
IN THE
UNITED STATES

She found Tanner—actually, she nearly collided with him—as he was leaving her bathroom with a wrench in his hands. "Your hot-water pipes won't scream anymore," he told her.

"I . . . thank you." She took the wrench he handed her and thought, *Here we go again*. One look at him and heat sucked low in her stomach, her breasts tightened, and she had the sudden fierce wish to be blond, small and adorable. "You must have made the stew?"

His voice was husky and low, his gaze drifting unreadably over her face. "Sure, I could see you were busy out there. It was pretty obvious you'd need more than a fast sandwich when you got in."

She gave him a thorough once-over. "That eye's gorgeous. I wouldn't mind a shirt that shade of purple."

"I would," he said dryly.

"The rest of your face doesn't look more than dented. And your color's back. Pity. Last night when you were dead gray, you could have done a tremendous job auditioning for a ghost." She watched his lips twitch and was relieved she hadn't offered him concern. Tanner would have spit it back, and as it was he looked like an intimidating giant in his doeskin vest and jeans. He smelled like clean soap and a fresh shower, and a lock of damp hair fell on his forehead. Exerting tremendous self-control, she refrained from pushing it back. "You earned your lunch doing all those chores. And you must be hungry."

"I should be going," he said immediately, and then stiffly, "I owe you thanks for putting me up. It seems this is the second time. I never meant to put you to that kind of trouble, much less put you out of your bed."

"Trouble? You're lucky I haven't roped you down and hired you on. Anyone who could take the scream out of that hot-water pipe *and* make stew that smells like sin, has definitely reached white-knight status in this house." She added, "If you can't stay, of course you can't. But there's certainly enough lunch for two."

When he hesitated, she was sure he wouldn't stay. She could see he was all right. Maybe he was bruised up, but he was walking straight and clear-eyed. Maybe too clear-eyed. His focus concentrated on her face with an odd searing intensity, and then he surprised her with a slow, "I'd stay for a quick lunch—if I wouldn't be in your way."

She made sure that didn't happen by making him pour the coffee and set the table. He looked startled when he first started ordering him around, but only a lazy man liked being waited on. Tanner was obviously used to doing, not sitting idle, but she had to hide a smile when she saw his big hands clumsily folding the napkins in the same way she'd folded them the first night he'd eaten here.

"This okay?" His voice was as gruff as scratchy wool.

"Just fine." She felt charmed that he'd remembered such a small thing, and touched that he cared about pleasing her. She put a ladle in the stew and carried it to the table. "The man who was outside with me was Wes Small. He's the retired vet, I don't know if you know him? Anyway, I picked his brain about George while he was here."

He ate three helpings, which didn't surprise her; his stew was excellent. Watching him relax was the shocker. The hard lonely eyes reflected light. He stretched out a leg. It took her a while to comprehend the impossible: Tanner wanted to be here. With her. And whether he wanted to or not, he was relaxing.

"I had a little talk with our owl yesterday about his housekeeping habits. I explained to George that I understood his desire to hoard food—we all like to lay up for hard times. But it's about the smell. For every two mice I give him, he hides one away for a rainy day. Now, I want to give him enough to eat, but for heaven's sakes!"

She had it then. Not a belly laugh, but definitely the growl of a low sexy chuckle. The sound disarmed her less than the look of him. Tanner's austere features lost their harshness when he laughed, when he forgot about being watchful and controlled. A man was too serious either because that was his nature or because he had to be. *I think you like to laugh, Tanner, and I think you need to. In fact, I think it would take nothing at all to...*

Before her exuberant imagination got her into trouble, she jumped up and started foraging for desserts. "Okay, we have apple pie. Day old, one piece. Somewhere around here I know I have oatmeal cookies and there's Oreos—"

"Oreos."

She glanced back. "You have it bad, don't you?"

"Bad?"

"Tanner, your tone was near rabid, and two other times I noticed you dented my supply. When you've got it that bad, it's hard to keep an addiction secret."

"It's not an *addiction*."

"What would you call it?"

"A desperate, uncontrollable, insatiable vice."

She could see that. Just like a kid, he bit the top off two cookies to make a double-white Oreo sandwich, while she started relaying Wes's advice. "Wes said you did a great job on the wing, and it should heal up fine, assuming we can keep George from pecking at the tape. He gave me some stronger stuff to use for a sling . . . I also asked him about the whole problem of captivity."

"Meaning?"

She closed her teeth around an oatmeal cookie. "I was worried whether we were hurting him. Like whether he could forget to hunt after being hand-fed. Or whether there was a danger of his becoming over-attached to us so that he couldn't survive in the wild again."

"And what did the vet say?" Behind her, Tanner carried dishes to the sink.

Her tone was wry. "That I could stop worrying. No one's ever going to tame a Great Snowy. Humans have been their genetic enemy for too long, and their instinct to hunt is too strong. He should have no problem taking to the wild again and—I forgot to tell you! You know what Wes said about their mating habits?"

It was taking less and less to get a smile out of Tanner. "Tell me."

"He said the female Snowy is shy, so when the male comes courting he brings her a gift. Maybe food, like a mouse or a shrew. The male Snowy will show the lady his courting gift, then hide it under his wing. Then show her. Then hide it again. That's how he gets her to trust him. If she wants the present, she has to come to him." Her eyes glinted humor. "It's hard to

picture George so romantic. All he does is look at me
with daggers. Lord, he's ornery!''

"Not with his own," Tanner said quietly. "He'd
fight anyone or anything to the death who dared to
threaten his mate or young. He's not supposed to trust
people. He can't. It could mean his life.''

"You know a lot about them, don't you?''

"Some.''

Too much she thought. He understood that owl too
well. She guessed that he'd protect his own just that
fiercely...and that someone had taught him some hard
lessons about trusting people. The streaks of white in
his hair added, not substracted, from his striking
looks, but they were definitely premature. A man
didn't turn white at his age from napping in front of
Saturday-afternoon football on T.V.

"Charly?''

He said her name at the end of a breath, as if it
wouldn't wait. She pivoted to face him, only his attention had been momentarily diverted by the glass jar
on her counter. "What on earth is this?''

"Just what it looks like. Honey with rose petals
floating in it. It stays like that for twenty-four hours,
then I sieve it. It's rose honey.''

"Rose honey," he echoed, and his eyes swept over
her face in a way that made her pulse tumble and her
nerves strain. Yes, she made rose honey and raised
orchids and liked lace next to her skin. He already
knew more about her than any other man ever had. He
knew too much. She'd risked too much...all for a
stranger with eyes so lonely she couldn't stand it. But
there was a limit. If he was going to make fun of her...

"I've been waiting since you came in for the third degree," he said quietly.

She wiped the last dish while he stood there in the doorway, halfway between his coat and her. She guessed he was ready to bolt. That made two of them. "You figured I'd ask you a whole pile of questions about last night?"

"I think most women would have. In fact, I can't think of any woman who would have unlocked her door and taken me in last night without some definite answers—answers about who I was, what I do, how my face came to look like a tire track and whether I was in trouble with the law. And your door was not locked, Charly."

"I told you it wouldn't be." She tucked the leftover stew in the refrigerator and straightened up. "You know something? No one thinks anything of a man living alone. No one thinks anything strange if a man chooses a life with a little adventure, a little challenge. I'm not talking about political equality here, I'm just talking about natures. Women seem to naturally tend toward a safer life. Only when I was a kid, Tanner, I never wanted to be safe...I wanted to be starting pitcher for the Minnesota Twins."

"Charly—"

She shook her head. "You wanted to know why I didn't ask you questions, so give me the chance to tell you. I'm not frail, I'm not fragile, and I'm not afraid—never have been—of life. I may raise orchids, but I also shot a black bear when I was nineteen, and I liked that flow of adrenaline, the risk, even the scare." She took a breath. "I respect people who don't put me down because I'm a woman and I need those things. And I respect other people who do what they need to do, Tanner. There is nothing I need to know about you that you haven't already told me in a dozen ways.''

He was silent a long time, and then he disappeared from sight. She heard him in the back hall, heard the shuffle of his boots, the zip of his jacket. Odd, but she didn't move at all while he prepared to leave. She just kept thinking that she'd done it again. Exposed herself. Told Tanner things that she didn't tell other people or even thought to.

When he reappeared in the doorway, he was pulling on his heavyweight arctic gloves, and his gaze settled gravely on her face. ''Starting pitcher for the Twins, hmm?''

He was working real hard not to grin. ''What kind of a career goal was that?'' He shook his head disgustedly. ''When I was a kid, I wanted to be a running fullback for San Francisco. Now *that's* a career goal.''

She burst out laughing, but far too quickly the devil left his eyes. He stopped fussing with his gloves and just stood there. ''I love to hear you laugh, Charly, more than you know and maybe too much.''

She had the strange sensation of waiting at the top of the first roller coaster track and looking down. ''I don't understand.''

''I have too little I can share. Too little I can offer a woman. Too few promises I can make.'' He said softly, ''I'm telling you to kick me out. For your sake. Just tell me, right now, not to come back.''

"What I'll *tell* you is to lighten up, Tanner. What is this? I think you've had too many Oreos. Come back if you want to. Don't if you don't. That's nothing to make into anything complicated."

He stared at her a long time, and then he was gone. From the window she watched him striding through the snow toward the road and felt her heart thump harder than a dog's wagging tail.

She put a stop to the cavorting heartbeats. From the first, Tanner had drawn her like bad news, like playing hooky, like sliding bare skinned into a cool smooth pond when you knew you were supposed to be mucking stalls. Tanner had the gift of making her feel a little wicked. If she let her overactive romantic imagination run wild, she'd have herself believing he was trying to tell her he cared.

She knew better than to invite such foolishness. Tanner was a lonely man who craved some company. He wouldn't be the only lonely man who'd wiled away a few hours in her kitchen. Men were always drawn to Charly for the same kinds of reasons, and she was bright enough to know that none of those reasons would ever hold a man like Tanner. She also knew that he could hurt her. Hard and maybe irreparably. If she let him.

Are you going to let him, Charly?

Resolutely she straightened and padded off to her greenhouse. She needed a solid hour of good clean dirt under her fingernails. Work had to be the antidote. She needed a sure antidote because she seemed to be falling, extremely unwisely, in love with him.

Charly, don't do that. Please don't. All you have to do is look in the mirror to know you'd be making a fool of yourself. He's traveled worlds you've never seen. If you're that hot to take on some pain, try a plain ordinary man. Not him. Anyone but him....

Six

***

He hadn't laid a finger on her, had he? If he kept his hands to himself and never stayed longer than an occasional hour, Tanner couldn't think of a single reason why he couldn't see her now and then. She could use someone to do a little unobtrusive watching over her. He'd manage to sneak in a few chores for her. And there was George.

Interesting logic, Tanner. Pity it isn't worth spit. Because if you're going to see her, you know darn well you're not going to keep your hands off her.

"Can you see what I'm talking about here?"

Tanner had been staring at the map Evan had spread on the polished desk. He just hadn't focused on it yet. Now he forced himself to.

The map looked as if someone had carelessly spilled blue ink over it, primarily because water dominated both the American Boundary Waters Canoe Area and the Canadian Quetico Provincial Park. As Tanner well knew, the American BWCA had been designated a true wilderness area, and Quetico had a matched set of protective laws.

Evan used a pencil for a pointer. "We know these areas have been used as meeting points. Rangers on both sides have found the snowmobile tracks. We know what's going on. The trick is stopping it."

"No regularity to where they're going in and coming out?"

"A certain regularity—they've avoided all eighty-three legal entry points by miles," Evan said dryly. "They know darn well we can't stake out twenty-four hundred miles of wilderness, and where they've got us—as you know—is because of our laws. It doesn't matter if you're the FBI or the Canadian Mounties or God. You can't use motors. They've got moving transportation while we're stuck on foot." Evan rolled up the map and handed it to him. "And the best time to catch them is when they're in that area, because that's when they're vulnerable. Once they're out, they've got organized help and a transportation system on their side. It's too late."

"All right." Tanner automatically shot off a series of clipped questions, fast enough to make his boss smile. He was caught. Whether Tanner wanted to or not, he could feel the pull of adrenaline, the taste of challenge, the need to be involved. And even as he peppered Evan with questions, he felt the brush of helplessness. His commitment to his work refused to disappear. He didn't know how to change his whole nature.

The briefest thought suddenly teased, worried, tantalized him. *She'd understand.* Not that he'd ask her to, but if there was a woman alive who accepted a man as he was, it was Charly.

Even after he'd reached for his jacket, Evan kept talking. "The Canadians are running a little touchy about this. They like it better when the bad boys are on the American side. The last thing they want is a public incident."

"You have something to tell me that I don't already know?"

Evan rocked back on his heels. "No backup."

"That's not new."

"Both sides'll be after your behind if they spot your plane."

"Maybe I won't use the plane."

"If you use anything with a motor—"

"Yeah, I know. I'll be breaking the law," Tanner said dryly.

Through the smoke haze of a thin brown cigarette, his boss studied him, and then with elegant white fingers stubbed out the butt in a crystal ashtray. "She's good for you."

Evan hadn't surprised Tanner in years. "I beg your pardon?"

His boss fussed with his shirt cuffs. "You've always had the judgment, Tanner. The judgment, the intelligence, the drive, the ability. But if you had a flaw, it was in a slight disregard for your own skin. She's muted that. You'll be more careful. Must be one of those ironies of fate, because very shortly physical danger is going to become the last of your priorities."

"You may be following this conversation, Evan, but you lost me," Tanner said dryly.

"Not long ago you gave me the definite impression that you wanted off the front line," Evan reminded him. "Did the obvious never occur to you? I have the same problem. I'll be sixty-seven next year, and if you didn't have a head harder than a petrified redwood, you would have figured out a long time ago that I was grooming you for my job."

In good time, Tanner sank in the nearest leather chair. His hand kneaded the back of his neck as he studied his boss.

"Don't waste your time looking surprised," Evan advised. "You were always good as a troubleshooter and your talents were always wasted. You know exactly what the border problems are, you've worked with every agency involved, you know international law as well as I do. Liaison work was the natural next step for you, and for the record, both the American and Canadian governments have already approved you as my replacement."

"Was anyone going to get around to asking me?" Tanner shook his head. "There has to be some humor here. I ask you for an out. Instead of an out, Evan, you're proposing to tip me out of the frying pan and into the fire." And an image of Charly burned in his mind. If it was unfair now to involve a woman in this job, Evan had just complicated that a dozen times.

His boss's sharp gaze never left his face. "It would hardly be an overnight transition, and I'm not asking you to make up your mind overnight. The end of January, though, there's a meeting scheduled at the house on Rainy Lake. It would be an ideal occasion for you to meet your core network of contacts from both sides.''

''Maybe you could slow down a minute.'' Tanner frowned. ''You're giving me a month—''

''Yes. To decide whether you want your total out. Or whether you want in so deep there'll never be another chance.'' Evan murmured, ''Think carefully, Tanner. Because that's exactly the way it has to be.''

Tanner lurched from the chair. ''I can give you my answer now.''

''I won't take it now.'' Evan's voice was thoughtful, calm, easy. ''You think you want to say no, but I think you're crazy if you believe you'll ever shake the commitment. It's part of your blood, it's part of your mind. And if she doesn't understand that—if you can't trust her to accept what you do—then she's the wrong woman.''

Tanner buttoned his jacket and reached for the rolled map. ''That's the second time you've brought up this 'she' business. If there was a woman in my life, Evan, hell'd burn before I'd drag her into my job.''

''Tanner?''

''What?'' He'd already stridden toward the door and had his hand on the knob.

Evan said patiently, ''Hell might just burn if you don't. She's had you tied in knots for weeks now. You think I'm too old to remember what that was like? Just be careful that she's the right one. She has to do more than accept who you are and what you do. She has to be strong, she has to be sure, she has to be there when the fire's so hot you think you're ready to call it quits.''

"You're not describing a woman, you're describing a saint," Tanner snapped.

"Well, hell." Evan's tone rolled with humor. "That's understood. It would take a saint to love you. Now would you kindly get out of here? Go solve our little drug problem in the BWCA. We'll talk when you get back."

Four days later, Tanner stuck his cross country ski poles in the crusted snow and paused for a rest. The midafternoon sun held no warmth but offered a blaze of brightness. The sweep of field marking Charly's border property was a diamond blanket.

Behind him were her backwoods. He'd just skiied the spread of pines and white paper birch on the assumption he'd find solitude. He'd been wrong. Her woods were loaded with tracks: deer, rabbit, raccoon, wolf, fox. Tanner was surprised there wasn't a traffic jam. Everybody wanted to be around Charly.

So did he.

He'd spent the past four days camped in blizzard conditions in the BWCA. The job hadn't been hard. The four city gentlemen weren't used to wilderness or blizzards. They may have started with the mistaken idea that northern Minnesota was a fine place to transfer drugs, but Tanner had politely encouraged them to change their minds.

Ten years before, he'd have called the job fun. These days he valued challenges that mattered more. And to add to his disgruntled mood, he'd come back to a growl of an argument with Evan. His boss wanted him to take that promotion. Ask him, and no one else but Tanner had the direct experience, the understanding of the area and its uniqueness to take Evan's job. They'd argued about that job, and somehow—because his boss was an unprincipled son of a seadog—they'd ended up arguing about Charly.

Evan had figured out, with merciless speed, that the only thing preventing Tanner from jumping for his job was a woman.

Evan also had very different ideas than he did about what a man could and couldn't ask a woman to be involved in.

Tanner had left the meeting that morning furious and on edge. Four hours later he'd still been furious and on edge when he'd strapped on his skis. There were no answers, not that he could live with. He was sick of thinking about the job. He was sick of thinking about what he had to do, what he needed to do.

He just wanted to see her.

Not to talk to her. Not to make things right that couldn't be right. Just . . . to see her. He picked up his ski poles, preparing to shove off again, when he spotted a blur of color on the white knoll in the distance. The blur became two Belgians, red and full-bodied and strong, and they were prancing pretty high through the snow, their hooves kicking up white and their heads held high and sassy.

Although the horses were still hundreds of yards away, they were trotting in his direction. The sun made such dazzling reflections on the snow that at first he couldn't make out the strange black contraption they were pulling behind them. When he did, he had the odd disarming sensation of being caught in a time warp.

The "black contraption" was an old-fashioned sleigh, the kind with runners and a flat cushioned seat that the pioneers had used a hundred years before. The woman driving the sleigh could have climbed out of the same time period.

She had a blanket on her lap. Her cheeks were pink and she wore no makeup. The braids pinned around her head added to the old-fashioned look, and Tanner wondered vaguely why he'd ever thought her plain. She was obviously beautiful. More than beautiful. She was crazy, out like this with the temperature near zero, carting the sleigh God knows where and for what. But he couldn't stop thinking that it was just like Charly, like her lace and her orchids and her singing love songs to his owl.

She slapped the right rein the moment she spotted him. "Hi, Tanner!"

That was like her, too. She couldn't have been expecting to see him, yet her greeting was as free as the shy welcome in her eyes.

He'd been battling the truth for four days now, yet a new version of truth now hit him with the stun of a sharp blow. Just possibly a man could do anything— not just what he had to do but *anything*—if that solace of a smile and "Hi, Tanner" were waiting for him.

He had no time to think that through. She slowed her Belgians with a "whoa" as she neared him. "Don't just stand there trespassing, Tanner. Get up here! I need some help!"

To hell with Evan, jobs, blizzards, conscience. He found his mouth shaping a grin. "What help? How's our owl? And where on earth did you get the sleigh?"

"George—your George, don't give me that 'our' nonsense—is rude, bad tempered and mean. We're starting to get along. He just hasn't realized it yet. As far as the sleigh, my dad had it saved in the top of the hay barn for years. My mother used to say dad would save chicken bones if she let him. We're talking about a man who never threw out holey socks just in case they could be used for something sometime." She moved across the sleigh seat, making room for him. "Just throw your skis in the back and get up here."

"All these orders. Where's the fire?" But he rapidly unclamped his skis and stashed his poles in the back. "And what's this ax for?"

"The obvious—cutting down a tree. Don't you ever look at a calendar? It's a week before Christmas. And I can cut down my own tree—heaven knows I've been doing it for years—but where I need help, desperately, is in the area of advice."

"Desperately, hmm? Why do I have the feeling I'm letting myself in for a lot of grief? Maybe you'd better tell me what you need, Charly."

He hauled himself up next to her on the sleigh seat, and the sense of time warp immediately intensified. Christmas trees...he couldn't remember the last time he'd had one. He knew life as a danger and a hunt and lonely vigils in the night, but he didn't know how to have a foolish conversation with a woman. Charly was obviously not in a mood to have any other kind.

She was antsy with excitement. Snowflakes stung her eyelashes and her eyes were as bright as green glass. "This is the problem, Tanner." she said darkly. "What I need is an eight-foot Christmas tree. What I'm about to pick out is a twelve- or thirteen-foot

Christmas tree. I always do. They always look nice and small in the woods, but the bottom line is when I'm trying to stuff them through the doorway at home. Just once—*once*—I want a tree smaller than Goliath. And all you have to do is make me see reason. That doesn't sound so hard, does it?''

''Charly?''

''What?''

''It's going to be a little tough to pick out a tree if you're driving away from the woods.''

The sun put diamonds in her grin. ''Of course. But we need a little spin first.''

She didn't want a little spin; she wanted to fly. The Belgians were in the mood for a fast trot, and the sleigh runners made a skimming hiss, moving as slick as skates on a mirrored ice pond. His knee rocked against hers when the horses took a hill. It was all so simple. The silence and snow and sun, the innocence of her laughter, the mischief in her eyes when she took a curve too fast, her cheeks burning red and her taking another hill. He didn't play like this. He didn't laugh, not the kind of laugh that started in the belly and roared in the wind, and he could have sworn that nothing in his life could ever be this simple again.

When she pulled the sleigh to a stop at the woods' edge, she threw off the blanket and briskly leaped from the seat. He was still breathing hard and braced for another death curve and laughing. ''What have you done to my spine, woman?''

''Realigned your vertebrae, did we? Isn't it a great sleigh?''

''Yes.''

"What do you think of that tree?" She motioned to a pine, then reached over the back of the sleigh for her ax.

"I think it's about fifteen feet tall."

Carrying her ax like a miniature female Paul Bunyan, she circled her choice of tree, then glanced at him. "But perfect. No bald spots. No hollows. Straight trunk. I changed my mind about wanting a small tree."

"Honey, you'd be lucky if that one fit in your barn."

She only had eyes for the one pine. "I have a lot of lights, a lot of bulbs. I don't like Christmas trees that are nice and neat. I like 'em cluttered and sagging and loaded with tinsel. I can't use a small tree."

"A half hour ago, you swore that was what you wanted."

She shrugged. "That was a half hour ago. Before I saw this one. I knew the minute I saw it that it was perfect." She handed him the ax. "I can smell the roasted chestnuts now. I hate roasted chestnuts, always have. *What* are you doing?"

He'd thrown down the ax and was advancing toward her. Her cheek was cold where he touched it. Her eyes were bright where he looked. She was bundled up like a snowman and boot-stomp shivering, and her lips were as stark red as cherries on snow.

When he swept her up and crushed his mouth on hers, a stark memory of Evan's words assaulted him: *The right woman needs to be stronger than you.*

He buried his hands in her hair and savored that silky texture. No woman could be less tough than Charly. That was exactly what made her wrong, exactly what made her right. His whole damn life was tough. He'd never minded that, never even thought about it, until she'd teased him with the treasure of softness.

Her cold lips heated for him. Her lashes fluttered down and her breath came in frantic little gusts, and then she stopped breathing, and so did he. He'd been doing fine until he met her. Now he hurt and seemed to be hurting all the time. She was the reason, her Christmas tree and her orchids and that irrational, whimsical, feminine side of her.

She didn't know. She just didn't seem to know what she offered a man. So he showed her, by whispering kisses on her jaw, on her nose. He lifted her high and hard against him, and when she started breathing in trembly little puffs, he kissed her again. Deeply. Thoroughly. In the end, as fiercely as the most primitive man staking a claim.

She wasn't looking so sassy when he finally raised his head. Her color was gone and her eyes dazed; she looked vulnerable and—so unlike Charly—a little scared.

He cupped her face between his two big gloves, looking at her, feeling more helpless than he'd ever felt in his life and not liking the sensation in any way. "Honey, I want you. You know that." He exhaled a gust of air that promptly froze. "I never had a problem with willpower until I met you. There's no way this is a good thing for you. All you have to do—all you ever had to do—was tell me to get out of your life. I'm telling you as honestly as I know how. If you don't do that, we're both going to run out of chances."

Stunned color climbed up her cheeks. Maybe he expected the anxiety, but not the surprise. Charly couldn't possibly doubt he wanted her. Hell, each time he'd come on to her with the finesse of a bull, and her response had been as volatile as his. The tension climbing between them was as easy to read as a first-grade primer.

Her surprise bewildered him, but not as much as her answer. When she lowered her head, her lashes shadowed the expression in her eyes and she quickly, blithely ducked away from him. "The only thing we're running out of chances on is getting this tree cut down while we still have daylight. If we don't get moving—"

"Charly—"

"The tree," she said stubbornly.

Charly made him do more than cut down the tree. She made him drive the sleigh back, then tend to George while she took care of the horses. Dusk had long fallen by the time she was making dinner, and Tanner, poor baby, was stuck working under her yard light with a tree that couldn't possibly fit in her house without an enormous amount of trimming.

The whole house smelled like pine the minute he brought it in. She fed him and then put him back to work, discovering that he could mutter as many swear words as her father in the process of hauling eight giant boxes of Christmas decorations down from the attic.

It was necessary to have a fire in order to decorate the tree. It was also necessary to have hot mulled cider and to pop corn to string. Tanner didn't understand all these necessary things. She put everything on a tree—bulbs and sun catchers and ribbons and berries, fragile antique ornaments and splashes of tinsel—he didn't understand that, either. She kept taking things out of boxes—wreaths and candles and music boxes and little glass houses that made snow when you shook them—until her living room was unwalkably cluttered and had the look of total devastation.

By nine o'clock a small fire crackled in the hearth. The tree lights winked on fallen bits of tinsel and glitter. The scents of rose and bayberry mixed with pine. Charly was sitting Indian style on the only space of carpet that wasn't cluttered. In her hand was a needle and thread and a two-foot rope of popcorn that would have been a lot longer if Tanner didn't keep stealing kernels from the line.

Maybe Tanner had intended to stay this long. Maybe he hadn't. Charly had fed him three glasses of mulled cider and kept him too busy to think. One thing was sure. He'd never seen such a mess. "All this for a couple of weeks? You have to be nuts. You know you're going to have to put it all away again on the first of January."

"Of course, at which time I'll rant and rave about never fussing so much again. But I always do. How can you do Christmas halfway? Tanner, the angel is leaning right."

"I just fixed it. You said she was leaning left."

"She was. Then. She still looks drunk. Can't you do something?"

He did something. He muttered something pithy about women just before he took down the angel and put up a star. "All right. What now?"

"Now you do something clever with the fire. I need a quiet bed of coals to roast chestnuts. We'll have to watch them. They can explode."

"I thought you didn't like chestnuts."

"I'm not fond of the taste. I love the smell. You can't beat the smell of roasting chestnuts."

"Charly..." Tanner stepped down from the step-ladder by the tree and mussed her hair en route to the fire. "I do not understand you."

That made two of them, she thought a little desperately. There was a level where she knew exactly what she was doing. There had been no turning away the man in the black-and-white flannel shirt hunkered down by the fire. Tanner was so hungry—for a home, for traditions, for someone to argue with about angels. An hour before she'd caught him shaking the snow in a little glass house, and he'd flushed red as a brick. Tanner? As embarrassed as a schoolboy? How she'd loved that look on his face.

She poked her needle through a popcorn kernel and missed, hitting her finger and drawing blood. When she sucked the finger, she had a sudden view of her oldest jeans—patched at both knees—and an ancient pair of argyle socks with a hole in the right toe. Her braid had long sneaked loose from its rubber band. Refugees looked sexier than she did.

Tanner had developed a problem with his vision in the past few hours. He kept looking at her. He'd looked at her before, of course, but not like this. Not with open possessiveness, with subtle appreciation, not with...desire. Possibly he'd suddenly become myopic, but he also kept in touch—a muss of her hair, the barest stroke of her shoulder, palm drifting over her fanny.

As a result, her whole body was aroused and had been for hours, like a light bulb switched on and forgotten. Her pulse was reckless, her skin oversensitive, her breasts tight and feverish.

If there was ever a man who needed someone, it was Tanner, but somehow she'd never believed he wanted her. Yes, he'd stolen kisses, but he was a lonely and troubled man. What was she supposed to do? Leave him alone out in the snow? And something rare and huge and special had filled her when he'd kissed her in the woods, when he'd spoken of wanting her. Like the slow fill of a helium balloon, she'd had the elated thought she could matter to him, that she could help him.

That balloon had long popped. She wasn't naive. She certainly understood what she'd invited when she asked him in, only in the woods she'd been extraordinarily high on loving him. She'd forgotten pride, forgotten a woman's fear of making a fool of herself, forgotten what she looked like, who she was.

Now those nasty little details dominated her mind.

Now, for every popcorn kernel she sewed, she nearly had a matching pincushion in her fingers because of her growing nervousness.

The smell of roasted chestnuts filled the room. Tanner lifted them with tongs onto a foil plate. In too much of a hurry to try one, he burned his finger. She was distracted enough to chuckle.

"They're delicious," he told her. "Why don't you like them?"

"I like them fresh from a tree, just not when they're roasted. They turn sweet."

"But that's exactly why they're good." He juggled a few in his hands like hot coals and edged down beside her. "I'm waiting, Charly," he said deliberately.

The needle darn near went through her finger. "What for?"

"Don't tell me you've finally run out of chores? Crooked angels. Untangling lights. Chestnuts."

"You get a break for chestnut eating. House rules. Hey!"

Before she could blink, he stole her popcorn rope and dragged it to the tree. With his mouth full of chestnuts, he said, "You get a break, too. More house rules. This thing's long enough."

"The needle's still in it!"

"It won't be." When he finished draping it around the branches, he stood back to inspect. "How does it look?"

"Like a hound dog's jowls. I hate to disappoint you, but you have no hidden talents as an interior decorator. The idea is to drape, not sag."

"Talk about your ungrateful women. Here I've done all this work and all I get is grief." Hands on hips, he swept the room with his gaze. "And at first look, the work's not done. We still have cleanup...but that'll have to wait."

"I agree. Sit down and relax with another mug of cider."

He was no longer looking at the room but at her. She thought of his Great Snowy, whose bright metallic eyes could stare with relentless, deliberate, unceasing intensity.

"I'm afraid," Tanner said slowly, "that relaxing will have to wait, too. You and I have a problem to solve. Right now. In fact—immediately."

Seven

——

I don't know what problem you're talking about," Charly said carefully.

"You. You're the problem." Tanner's eyes had the shine of ebony. "Come here, honey."

She never had the chance to move before he strode toward her, looking tall and powerful and very dark with the tree lights blinking behind him. In one smooth motion he grasped her hands and pulled her to her feet.

She instinctively braced for a pass that never happened. His arms folded around her and he tucked his chin on top of her head and hugged. Hard. A pass was a pass and a hug was a hug. This was a clear-cut, totally unexpected, snugly warm hug. For Tanner to offer affection was both delicious and precious and Charly wanted to savor it for just those reasons.

Unfortunately, she felt as if she'd just plugged into an electric chair.

"Feel better?" he murmured. "You've been jumpy as a cat for the past hour. It took me a while to realize what was wrong, because I'd never seen you nervous before." His chin rubbed the top of her head. "I'm on my way out the door, Charly, so you can let that bundle of nerves relax. I'm your problem, aren't I? Which is almost funny, because I've done my damnedest to make you afraid of me from the day I met you. But not for this, foolish one. Never for this. You can't believe I'd hurt you. You can't believe I would ever force you into doing anything you didn't want to do. I never meant for you to feel threatened. I—"

"For God's sake, Tanner. Would you just shut up and kiss me?"

A log chose that moment to tumble and spark in the fire, which was a good thing because the rest of the room was suddenly silent as a tomb. Tanner's arms loosened their hold and his chin lifted from the top of her head.

The look of him sent a tremor up her spine. His thick dark hair was disheveled, his features taut, and his muscles coiled with the vital dangerous energy that was so much a part of him. There was something in his eyes, something unfathomably dark and rich and silver that should have made an untried woman run, and fast, for the nearest door.

She didn't run. With a first kiss, weeks ago, she'd had an image of a man who could break.

Now, for his sake, she stood absolutely still, even when she heard the low warning in his voice. "Charly, be careful what you invite. I know you're not sure. I..."

Sure? She was as sure as a reed in the wind, yet in slow motion her gaze took in a man's soft mouth and a man's dark lost eyes and a man's firelight-golden skin. Tanner's mouth, Tanner's eyes, Tanner's skin. And when she was all done looking, she framed his face in her hands and lifted up on tiptoe.

She had never loved a man like she loved him. She had never guessed a man could need her, not in the terrifyingly powerful way Tanner seemed to need her. So she mentally said an abrupt "to hell with sanity" and kissed him. Fire crackled on the surface of their skin the moment their lips molded together.

Tanner could be so harsh, so cold, so defensive. If she'd worried he could break, she'd never expected the simplest kiss to be his downfall. The look in his eyes spoke of reverence, and his mouth rubbed against hers with intimate tenderness. Her fingers climbed in his hair and she deepened the kiss, brazenly swaying closer so that breast could court breast, thigh court thigh.

Her heart warned her she was hurtling toward a dangerous abyss. She was throwing herself at a man who couldn't want her for a long-term relationship. She had no illusions about the future and was sure he didn't, either. She was just plain practical Charly, while he was... Tanner.

In her mind the differences between them were just that absolute. Yet despite past pride and past shame, she loved him. For this moment there just wasn't anything else, and her emotions tumbled toward that sweet dark abyss when she sensed his growing urgency. Quick kisses lengthened, blurred, fed one into the other. At the first touch of her tongue Tanner tightened like a bolt, yet his lips still scalded hers in return.

Her hands skidded down his hard muscles. His shirt was untucked, so her fingertips could easily search for his bare skin. Suddenly her palms were sliding over his warm supple flesh.

Tanner let out a groan like a man battling pain, and Charly made the extraordinary discovery that passion could be rich and reckless. She loved the sound he made, and nothing in her life had ever made more sense than this. She wanted the touch, sound, sight, smell and taste of him. All at once. Now. The romance of Tanner had always drawn her... his loner chip, his mystery, his striking looks and the dangerous quality about him. He was a renegade, a roguish knight, a pirate—those were the fantasies.

The real man was much more potent. Her stampeding pulse measured a building fear—a woman's terribly private fear of looking foolish, clumsy, laughable. She pushed aside the intrusive emotion and focused all her attention on Tanner.

Her fingertips found scars on his chest and ribs. They were the scars of a man who'd known more than his share of pain. Her lips absorbed the pressure and texture and taste of a man who definitely knew more about kissing than she did, but his mouth was no steadier than her own. Her gaze took in rugged features and unyielding bone... but his eyes were looking increasingly lost and wild. He needed. Badly. He wanted. Badly.

It had to be right. Maybe she didn't know what to do, maybe she didn't have the first clue about pleasing him, but she knew what she wanted. Tanner. Free. All guarding gone, all wariness gone, all tension gone, all loneliness and hurt and whatever else troubled him.

Courage built from that desire. Momentum fed from his volatile response to everything she did. The blind sense of her own feminine powers was new, but that was building, too. She'd never felt so sure, so strong... until her fingers slipped the button on his jeans.

Tanner reacted as though lightning had struck him. Roughly, irrationally, he swept her up in long strong arms and headed for the bedroom. For Charly, the blurred fog of a dream suddenly had edges. Sanity was as alarming as seeing the familiar crack in her hall ceiling moving above her. "Tanner, are you crazy? I can walk!" she whispered.

"You can do a lot of things that I never expected." He kissed her nose, right in the middle of the dark hall. "At least while I'm carrying you, one of us has a slight chance of regaining a little control. When a man has a hair-trigger response, it's called a problem. When a woman's in a hurry, it's called an unbearable delight—but damn you, Charly. I thought you were shy!"

He'd meant to tease, to make her smile, but the moment he laid her on the comforter and switched on her bedside lamp, he saw her stricken face.

"Did you want shy?" she asked carefully.

He wanted to hit himself over the head with the nearest brick. The same woman who'd just put his body through merciless, wild, uninhibited torture was now lying defensively still. The expression in her green eyes was fragile, and her mouth trembled.

He invited his galloping hormones to take a fast trip to hell and eased down next to her. "I want *you*, Charly. I've wanted you from the day I met you. Just as you were, just as I found you, just as you are."

"But you said—"

"I know what I said. Something stupid. And I misunderstood something terribly important, because I'm an extremely stupid man." He breathed deep and slow, forcing the clawing rawness of desire to mute, alter, refocus.

"You are not stupid."

"Yes, I am." He swept kisses all over her face, soft ones, light ones, tender ones. She began to relax until he started to undo her blouse buttons, and then, like a sprung trap, her hands closed on his wrists.

He kissed her wrists, her palms, her fingertips until her hold eased and her eyes closed and he could feel her heart stop hammering panic.

His beguilingly wanton Charly had clearly faked him out. He wasn't going to give her a chance to do that again, nor was there any way he was going to hurt her again. She was new to this. Painfully new. Maybe too new for a too-blunt, rough-edged, insensitive man who had never known anyone like Charly.

He had to make this right for her. Not just tonight, but what they were together and what they could be. Evan and honor, a man's commitments and his unreconcilable concerns about involving the lady in his life—none of that disappeared. It just diminished under the weight of a simpler truth. Charly mattered more.

Tomorrow that fierce, possessive, consuming truth would undoubtedly scare him. At the moment the lady beneath him had the sheen of desire in her eyes. She was also shaken and trembly, as close to fear as he ever wanted to see her. Her inexplicable fear perplexed but, even more, drove him. Charly needed taking care of. He didn't have time for anything else.

His lips took hers when he lifted her to peel off her blouse. He only severed the kiss long enough to deftly pull the scrap of pink silk camisole over her head. He would have liked to look at her in it. Instead his gaze never left her face, and her nerve seemed to drop on the floor with her abandoned camisole. She was swallowing, and the only color in her face was two streaks of pride on her cheekbones.

"Tanner, it may have been a while since—"

"That's okay," he whispered softly.

"Not that I don't know what I'm doing. I don't want you to think this is anywhere near my first time or anything ridiculous like that. For heaven's sakes, I'm thirty-two years old—"

"I know you are and I never thought any such thing," he lied.

"I'm well aware that some men don't care for a woman being aggressive—"

He nipped that one in the bud. "Honey, I like you wild and I like you shy and I like you *any* way you are." His voice had never been softer. "You like to fantasize, though, love? I'll bet you like to fantasize. Just for fun, you might like to close your eyes. Just for a minute, you might pretend you're feeling a little shy. Just because it feels good, you might like to imagine that you've never had a man kiss your breasts before, not like this."

She had beautiful breasts, smooth like cream, round and ripe like something out of a man's dream. Even before he touched them, they were swollen and sensitive. He lavishly teased her with a fingertip, then his palm. He cupped, cradled, kneaded...but always softly, always tenderly, always watching her until he couldn't wait any longer to dip his head.

Her nipples were like dark raspberries until his tongue praised their beauty, and then they tightened into taut little nubs. His lips closed on one tip, then the other. She tasted sweet and warm. She tasted like excitement, and the lady, he noticed, was getting restless. When he slid a jean-clad thigh between hers, her pulse began to ricochet. He kissed the spot between her breasts.

"I think you like this fantasy, Charly," he murmured. "I think you love pretending to be shy."

"I...yes."

"So maybe we'll take our fantasy just a little further, love." He kissed her closed eyelids and slid a palm down to her jeans button and zipper. She flexed every muscle. "Maybe you could even pretend you were a little scared, a little nervous," he murmured calmly. "Not *really* scared, because if there is absolutely anything you don't want me to do, we stop. Always. Anytime. You hear me?"

"I don't...want you...to stop." But her breath suddenly caught on his name. "Tanner?"

"Hmm?"

"Would you not look at my sock?"

The squeeze of humor in her voice was when he knew, absolutely, that he loved her.

As far as the hole in her sock, he'd already discovered that in between pulling off her jeans, his jeans, her socks, his socks. He'd seen holes in socks before. He hadn't seen Charly naked before, and once he skimmed off the ounce of pink lace covering her hips, he had her bare.

She stole his breath away. Naked, warm and hard, he slid back down beside her, letting his hands savor what his eyes were treasuring, the long, long legs, the satin cream breasts, the slim waist, the lush riot of silky blond hair between her thighs. Her fanny was small. So small he had the wicked masculine urge to bite each cheek. Gently. Sexily. He didn't do that. He didn't want to scare her; he didn't want her to know that desire was ripping through him like the winds of a hurricane.

But Lord, she was beautiful. Fresh, sweet, soft. Ripe. Her skin had the scent of roses. Her lips had the taste of everything he'd ever valued, ever needed in this life.

"Charly?" Bit by bit, she was eroding his sanity. He tried to keep his kisses gentle, but when she offered her tongue, there was a little more sanity gone. He wanted her to touch him, but when her slim white hands started to slide up his shoulders, he lost another major chunk. When she willingly arched beneath him, he couldn't breathe. "Honey, you're going to have to tell me...soon, love, real soon...exactly how shy you want to play this fantasy."

"I—"

"It's okay. I swear it's okay. Just talk to me."

She tried to, and he tried to quit kissing her so she'd have the chance, but that was hard. He was so aware that she was darn near ravenously kissing him back. He'd been positive the contact of his lean scarred bareness would tense her up again. He was wrong. The fire that had so blindly consumed Charly in the living room was making a comeback. A delicious, sweet, luring, dangerous comeback. He barely managed the words. "Close your eyes, love. Just tell me...what you want, what you need. What you're imagining..."

"Maybe, Tanner, maybe we could pretend like there was only one other time. And a long, long time ago. And maybe like it wasn't the best experience known to mankind."

A most unkind thought tore through Tanner that sometime, somewhere, there was a man he wanted to find. He just wanted a few minutes with him. Hell, he'd settle for five.

He abruptly banished every thought but Charly. The lamplight glowed on her face, on hollows and shadows and her dazed green eyes. Her arms wound around him when his palm eased down to the juncture between her thighs. She made a soft sound, a wild sound, when he discovered that sweet dampness. Her legs involuntarily clamped around him, not in shyness but in response.

His fingers stroked, teased, wooed. She tried to tell him something, her voice urgent and restless and hoarse, but he shushed her. He already knew what she wanted. The delight, the joy, was getting her there.

She found pleasure the first time, hot and powerful and blind, from the rhythm of his hand. The intimate ripples took her like fire, like the arc of lightning, like the whisper of a love song.

He soothed her afterward, stroking her hair, her cheek, tracing her bottom lip with his thumb. He couldn't stop looking at her and he couldn't stop touching her. Her passion had been released, not his, yet he had the oddest sensation of soaring.

Always, always, he'd been a man of the earth, a man tied to reality as he saw it, honor as he saw it, the harsh black and white of principles as he knew them. Those ties were unforgiving and unyielding. He'd accepted them a long time ago. They weren't a choice. They were simply how he saw life.

Not with her. Her lashes fluttered sleepily open and the way she looked at him, he could have touched sky. "Love?"

She was having such a hard time making her lips coordinate that she only barely managed a "hmm?"

"You are sinfully easy to please, Miss Erickson."

"Your turn now," she whispered.

But he shook his head. "I wasn't prepared. Not for you. Not for this." His thumb stroked her chin. "I'm not a fan of Russian roulette, not where risking a lady is involved. Never where risking you is involved, honey." Afraid he'd said too much, he added quickly, "And it doesn't always have to be two ways. I'm no teenage boy. We'll save another kind of lovemaking for another night."

Her eyes blinked wide then. Wide-awake wide. His shy lady, his wanton lady—he'd been damned if he'd yet figured out which Charly really was—abruptly shifted her weight over him. He felt the soft crush of her breasts, the feminine weight of her thighs against his. He saw her eyes, green as emeralds and almost as stubborn as her pride.

She kissed his brow, then his nose. "Possibly, Tanner, I'm not as skilled in this arena as you are." She flicked her tongue in the shell of his ear. "But I've learned a lot in the past two hours about creativity, and a lover's tact and inherent sneakiness."

"Sneakiness?"

"I wasn't shy. I was shook. Which you knew, damn you." His ear was sensitive, but not half as sensitive as the pulsing hardness pressed against her abdomen. "I can be sneaky, too. In fact, I've always had kind of a sneaky philosophy about men. Sneaky and simple. When a man's hungry, you feed him. When a man's tired, you put him to bed." She reached over his head to flick off the bedside lamp. "And when a man's on fire, you find some way to quench that flame." She murmured, "Don't hesitate to advise as we go."

"Charly?"

"Hmm?"

"You don't need any advice." A moment later he repeated "Charly?"

"Hmm?"

"I think you're *definitely* over your shyness."

Charly wakened alone, the spot next to her in bed distinctly abandoned. When she turned her head to read the bedside clock, she found a note taped over the dial. "Sleep until high noon, Charly. I'll take care of the horses."

Smiling, she peeled off the tape to discover it was eight o'clock. The same as a socialite's high noon, by Charly's standard, yet, for a moment longer, she fell back against the pillows and closed her eyes. She felt wickedly lazy. Decadently sensual. Stark raving beautiful and giddy as a kite in a high wind.

It was all Tanner's fault. They hadn't made love—not *totally* made love—yet she had the full measure of the lover. He was a secrets stealer. An inhibitions thief. A teaser of epic dimensions, a passionately exciting man who laughed in bed, a man who valued babies too much to risk them, a man who could be ruthlessly tender, intimately mischievous. Loving. Tanner knew loving as she'd only fantasized it.

She was still smiling when she forced her eyes open and climbed out of bed. She smiled through a fast shower, and she smiled through a plundering of her drawers until she came up with a red mohair sweater, jeans, socks. She smiled in search of her hairbrush, and her smile abruptly died when she faced herself in the dresser mirror.

You feel stark raving beautiful, do you, Charly?

The lady staring back at her wore a shapeless red sweater and had a fuzz of wild blond hair that never behaved. There were no model's high cheekbones, no sexy mouth, no dazzling deep-set eyes. She had straight teeth and clear skin, but the features added up to a face that made maiden aunts say, "You have the kind of beauty that comes from the inside, dear." Or worse. "Beauty is in the eyes of the beholder."

As a teenager she'd yearned for prettiness. As a grown woman she'd shelved vanity as a waste of time. Yet now she thought of Tanner's dark striking looks, his haunting gray-silver eyes. He was a man of courage and passion and power. He'd traveled worlds she never had or would. He had the experienced sexuality of a man who knew women and life.

And suddenly she ached, inside, outside, all over.

He's not for you, Charly. He was never for you. He needed someone last night and you were there. You're friend material. You've always been friend material, but as for attracting a man long-term . . .

When? When had she ever attracted a man? Much less one like Tanner?

Minutes later she let herself out into the gray dark morning. The sun hadn't risen yet. Clouds hung like low puddles in the sky, and snow gusted in spits and swirls. She tromped through the drifts as if a nightmare were after her, and maybe it was. Her worst fear had always been making a fool out of herself.

Now she couldn't wait to get to the barn and face him. She planned to smile. She planned a cheerful face and casual easy conversation. She planned to look as though she'd sloughed off last night for the short unplanned encounter it was, and above all she planned to be a friend. From the first day he'd started haunting her back door, she'd never doubted Tanner's need for a friend. She had no reason to believe he would have asked for more if she hadn't come on to him.

So fix it, Charly. Quit thinking, put your chin up and face him man to man.

Once she found him, though, she had a small problem with that scenario. Tanner wasn't downstairs but in the pigeon loft. At the sound of her boots on the stairs, he turned his head. One look and her man-to-man idea died a fast death. One look and Tanner aroused every feminine instinct she'd ever had—none of them remotely friendly—and all of them, at that moment, fiercely protective.

"Hey, you had orders to sleep in," he scolded her.

His tone was warm and easy—and fake. His hair was rumpled as though a hand had shoveled through it, not once but a dozen times. The glow of the lantern illuminated the grooved lines on his brow, the hollows under his eyes. A caged cougar couldn't look more spring tense, and his gaze locked on her face with a look that was haunted, hungry, tearing.

"I slept until eight as it was. Never could keep lazy hours," she said lightly, but she couldn't take her eyes off him. All she could think of was to heck with last night, with love, with pride. Something was eating Tanner alive. "You had to be up at dawn. I saw how you cleaned up the living room."

"I was getting to the horses, but not until I'd paid a quick visit to George."

"He's doing great, isn't he?" As much as she wanted to ask him what was wrong, her first impulse was to calm and soothe. Tanner was coiled tighter than the lid on a blasting cap, and every word he uttered was spoken carefully.

As she could have guessed, though, a comment about the Great Snowy diverted him. They both glanced at George, who seemed to have decided that two visitors were too much. Fluffing up his good wing, he paced his perch, bright yellow eyes glaring at them. The soft luster was back in his white feathers. He was magnificent and wanted them to know it. He was also hopelessly wary whenever anyone came close—exactly like Tanner, Charly thought fleetingly.

"I meant to mention it last night—I noticed the sling on his wing was new. You must have changed it, Charly."

"The devil and I are slowly coming to terms," she said. "He keeps trying to make me believe he's pure mean. I keep trying to make him believe he's pure scared." She grinned. "He'll close his eyes if I sing to him but I'm not sure if that's a sign of trust . . . or disgust."

She won a chuckle from him. "You're still spoiling him. I see you brought him a toy."

"The fake mouse? That wasn't a toy, Tanner. I was trying to give him something to hide so he'd quit hoarding the dead mice."

"Is it working?"

"No," she said wryly. "But he likes it. He picks it up in his beak and throws it at me whenever I come in. Then I hide it for him again. It's kind of become a game."

Tanner let himself out of the cage and glanced at her. "I would never have guessed he'd become tame enough to play games."

She thought that once upon a time she'd never expected Tanner to become tame enough to smile, or to laugh, or to gently, sensitively, passionately steal away the inhibitions of a woman who'd been hoarding them for years. "Are you hungry enough for breakfast?"

"I'll survive until after we both get through with your horses downstairs."

"You don't have to help—"

"The chores will be done that much faster if I do. Don't forget, I grew up around horses. I can handle a curry comb and a pitchfork. And after that ... you have anything planned for the afternoon?''

"Not really." Actually, she had a dozen things to do. Odd that she couldn't remember a single one. For a few minutes Tanner had seemed to relax. Not now. Other people showed nerves by tugging an ear, hand movements, fidgeting. Tanner's voice turned rusty and he got a look on his face that was forbidding, harsh and coldly intimidating.

She wished, desperately, that she had the right to hug him to bits. *And throw yourself at him again, Charly? Be a friend, damn you.*

"Well," he said finally, "if you haven't anything better to do..."

Still she waited, not quite sure why she was holding her breath.

"I thought I might take you over to see my place later in the afternoon."

She said easily, calmly, "Sure. That would be fine." But there was a lump in her throat as big as a golf ball. Gossip had it that no one had stepped foot on Tanner's property since he'd moved home. She never thought she'd hear the offer. She'd never expected it.

And she sure as heck had no idea how seeing his place could have any link to the weight of trouble in Tanner's eyes, but she would. She'd also get that look out of his eyes or die trying. "We'll have to take my truck." She tossed the words over her shoulder as she headed down the stairs. "If I remember right, you came here yesterday on cross-country skis. I'll bet they're still in the back of the sleigh."

Eight

———

Your mother obviously liked primitive antiques."
Charly glanced at him. "And books. I'd be hard-
pressed to believe you were the one who collected all
these romances, Tanner!"

"I didn't even know they were still there." By sheer
force of will, Tanner kept his voice calm. "I guess I
never looked at those shelves when I moved back in
the house."

"You don't mind if I look?"

The question only appeared innocuous. Tanner had
figured out about two hours ago that Charly was determined to drive him out of his mind. "Go ahead."

She smiled en route to the bookshelf. That smile
could distinctly unhinge any man's sanity, and his was
already teetering. The afternoon was not going *anything* like he'd anticipated.

He felt as if he were standing in the path of a semi, waiting for it to mow him down. The decision to bring her here hadn't been an easy one. Trust was no problem. If he couldn't trust Charly, he'd throw in the towel. But that wasn't the point. His place was a statement of who he was, what he did.

He'd brought her here to give Charly the chance to decide if she could accept who he was, what he did.

He'd already decided that she couldn't, which was why he had a clashing headache and a pulse-pounding feeling of dread. When push came to shove, he knew he'd find the strength to do the right thing. After last night, he knew he had to. Last night, Charly had come apart for him; she had been precious and real, sensitive in passion and exquisitely vulnerable.

Vulnerable was the word that kept gnawing at him. He wasn't blind. Charly cared for and was attracted to him. But did she feel love? He didn't think she was there yet. She didn't seem to be suffering the hangover symptoms he had—the permanent headache, the mood shifts from anxious to sky-high, the mind jittery on every other subject but getting his next fix. Of her.

She was the best thing that had ever happened to him, but the reverse was hardly true. He couldn't hurt her. Before she was any more emotionally involved, he had to offer her an honest out, and bringing her here had struck him as the easiest way to do that. If his place didn't put a label on his job, it was certainly a stamp of his life-style.

Like a man on an island with a tidal wave coming, he was waiting for the concern and worry to cross her face. For her to instinctively pull back an emotional distance. For her to express distress, wariness. The first sign of a negative reaction from her and Tanner had promised himself he would somehow find the strength of will to give her her out.

Only the darn woman wasn't giving him a chance to do the right thing.

When they'd driven in, he'd parked her truck next to his. She noted that his pickup had more state-of-the-art communication equipment than exceeded any man's hobby. But all she said was "You'd better not let me touch anything, Tanner. I'm allergic to anything electronic."

She'd taken off for the empty horse barns and bemoaned them for the waste of facilities they were. He got a lot of questions about the riding horses his mother used to raise and where he boarded his horse but received no comment on the land-seaplane parked next to the barn. It was common knowledge he flew backpacking summer tourists into the wilderness, of course. But it wasn't summer now and she could hardly fail to notice that the plane was outfitted with skis instead of pontoons, ready for use on the snow-cleared landing strip.

Maybe Charly didn't know about planes, so he'd taken her in the house. The brick ranch home had three bedrooms. One he slept in. The second was a study, with a wealth of books on international law, a ham radio strong enough to connect halfway across the world and a computer that wasn't used for video games. He used the third bedroom to store an arsenal of survival equipment: packs, lanterns, ropes, clothes, gear.

Charly had said, "You're disgustingly neat, Tanner. I don't even see any dust. You must go crazy when you're around all the clutter in my house."

He was going crazy, all right. He couldn't very well answer questions until she asked them. There was too much he couldn't tell her, but the equipment sprawled all over couldn't leave her many doubts that he was involved in something that nice men simply weren't. If he took Evan's offer, that was going to get worse, not better. Charly certainly didn't know that, but he'd shown her more than enough to disturb her.

The lady was not only undisturbed, she was having a wonderful time. She'd found the four bags of Oreos in the kitchen and teased him about being a hoarder like George. Somehow between the truck and the house she'd managed to get him tale-telling about his father's desertion when he was ten, the grief and the anger of a boy having to turn man overnight. Tanner never told anyone about that old dead history. Charly simply confused him.

She'd confused him more when she'd queried him about every jug and vase his mother had collected over the years. Heck, he had no idea what half of them were; he'd simply forgotten they were there. She loved the burnt orange color—she called it "pumpkin"—of the rug in the living room. She had also wildly enthused over the tall oak bookshelves and the Jenny Lind couch and the antique armoire, which she said was valuable.

Distractedly he squinted at it again, doubting he'd ever remember to call it an armoire instead of a cupboard, and then he refocused determinedly on Charly. He wouldn't be half so wrought up if she didn't keep diverting him with armoires. The look of her crouched by the bookshelves, unfortunately, was another hopeless diversion.

Her wild red sweater was so baggy it drew inevitable attention to her breasts. Her jeans sagged at the seat, partly because they were aged, mostly because Charly didn't have much of a seat. He loved that tucksmall fanny of hers. And she'd never had time to braid her hair that morning. He guessed now, though, why she wore it so often in braids. Her hair hung below her shoulders, fine as a whisper, silky... and wild. It tangled. It swished around her face. She pushed it behind her ear; in seconds it snuck free again.

He wanted his hands in that hair, that fanny, those breasts. He wanted to hold her and he wanted to be held. He couldn't do either and leave Charly free to make judgments she had to make. But if she didn't do something soon...

Abruptly she lifted her head from the bookshelves and smiled. "Did you realize? Your mom only picked romances with horses in them."

"Did she? I guess that's no surprise. I think in the long run she wanted to get into fancy breeds like you have, but she did okay with her mixed bloods, her saddle horses." If he shoved a hand through his hair one more time, it was probably going to stand permanently on end. "Charly—"

"I would have loved your mother, Tanner," she said softly.

"I *know* she would have loved you." Mentally he groaned. How could she keep doing this to him? Suddenly he couldn't shake the image of how much his mother would have loved Charly. He wanted to tell her that his mother had been one of a kind, strict with a switch, unrelenting about what she believed in, but uncompromisingly kind. Always, always, she'd been there for him. He wanted to tell Charly... Tanner straightened irritably. That was half the problem with loving the darn woman. He wanted to tell her everything, but not now. "Charly!"

"Could I borrow some of the books? Some of these are ancient, out of print. I'd never be able to find them now. Of course if you'd rather I didn't—"

"Honey, you can have every book on the shelf. Hell, you can have the bookshelf. And the armoire. And the whole damn room. But not today."

Charly raised startled eyes at his impatient tone and then crossed the room in four quiet strides. She patted his wrist. "I know what's wrong with you. A whole afternoon doing nothing, and you're undoubtedly hungry. How about taking a ride into International Falls for dinner? We could drive your fancy truck, maybe even take in a movie."

"Movie?"

"You know," she said calmly. "A movie's where you pay your money and they give you a little ticket, then you load up on buttered popcorn and slump in a chair with your feet up."

"Honey, we can't go to a movie right now."

The girl raced through the black night, dodging trees and tripping on branches. Her enemy was unseen except for the glitter of his long steel knife blade in the moonlight. He was gaining on her. Both were breathing hard. The girl stopped, clutching her side...

Charly reached for another handful of popcorn from the container in Tanner's lap. It had to be one of the worst horror flicks she'd ever seen. A lot of blood and guts but no plot. The girl couldn't act worth beans.

Her own performance, Charly considered judiciously, was far superior. Next to her, Tanner's big shoulders were scrunched low in the seat, his long legs lazily stretched in the aisle. His indolent posture was no accident. It had taken a prime rib dinner, a stroll through the mall and a dripping ice cream cone to get him this far.

The movie theater was all but empty, but the scattering of paired teenagers in front all gasped when the knife arced in the moonlight, then sank. Blood filled the screen. Next to her, Tanner yawned.

Smiling, Charly reached for another handful of popcorn and discovered the box was empty. She lowered it to the floor. Somewhere in their squash of jackets and scarves and gloves was a napkin. Her fingers were a sticky mass of butter and salt.

It didn't take a mind reader to figure out that Tanner hadn't taken in a simple movie—or gone out to a simple dinner or indulged in a frivolous ice-cream cone—in a very long time. From the look of his home, it had been ages since Tanner had indulged in any of the normal simple pleasures most people took for granted. And as of the moment they'd driven on his property, he'd seemed to be waiting for some kind of dramatic traumatic reaction from her.

Charly had never been much on drama or trauma. Tanner had been all but begging for a confrontation. He could have it, she was dying to talk to him, but not when he was verging on a near-shouting unreasonable mood. She figured she deserved an Academy Award performance for her role as tranquilizer.

Now, though, she was beginning to wish she had a real tranquilizer for herself. Tanner's earlier tight mood seemed to be catching. She couldn't sit still and she couldn't concentrate. Like a drift of wind, uneasy emotions tugged at her and then namelessly disappeared.

She tried to convince herself, at least for the next three minutes, that the hardest problem she had was finding a napkin for her popcorn-sticky fingers.

"What are you looking for, honey?" Tanner murmured.

Her heart responded to that "honey" with a little rolling clutch. She was trying, hard, to be a friend. She was trying just as hard to keep any foolish romantic notions at bay. Still, she had the sudden deplorable thought that she'd be stuck for the rest of her life associating the word *honey* with Christmas tree lights, the tastes of cider and Tanner, the feel of his bare skin and shivers chasing through her.

That, though, was her problem. Prosaically she whispered, "I'm looking for napkins. I know I brought some in from the concession..." Another brilliant splash of scarlet exploded on the screen. She gave up her napkin search and resigned herself to a trip to the washroom. Tanner's fingers suddenly wrapped gently, firmly on her wrist. She glanced at him.

"Just watch the movie."

A pair of wicked black eyes pounced on the screen. The villain. Madness amok. The devil uncaged.

She must have jumped two feet when Tanner's tongue skimmed the tip of her fingers. "Relax, Charly," he whispered.

She was willing to, she planned to, the very moment he released her wrist. Maybe the devil had a craving for butter and salt? Slowly, wickedly, he lapped the length of one finger, lingered in the valley and then lapped up the side of the next. His tongue was warm, wet, soft.

When he finished her fingers, he turned his attention to her palm. His tongue drew circles in her palm. Lavishly lazy circles. Delicious circles. Intimately private circles.

His focus never wavered from the movie screen. He acted as if he had no concept of the streak of madness he was inciting in Charly. He took the tip of her thumb in his mouth. She felt the softest graze of his teeth, the tease of his tongue. His lips sheathed her thumb tip, clamped hard, then withdrew. Sheathed, then withdrew. Sheathed, then withdrew.

She was suddenly breathing as though she'd just had a race with a train. All the colors on the screen looked like spun mist. Her bones had liquefied.

"Charly?" he murmured. "Honey, are you real interested in this movie?"

Her lips and tongue and vocal chords all moved, but it took two tries before they produced any sound. "What movie?"

He swooped up jackets and scarves and Charly and had them outside the theater on the short side of sixty seconds. Except for the movie theater, the mall was closed this late. The night lights of International Falls glowed from the distance. The silence was delicious.

Snowflakes fell like errant confetti from a pitch-black sky. A lone car driving by might have seen the tall dark man press the smaller blonde against the brick wall, but probably not.

Tanner made a point of stealing his kiss in the shadows. It wasn't the kind of kiss he wanted anyone to see. He took her mouth as if he'd have starved without it; he pushed aside jackets so the length of him could crush the length of her.

He hadn't touched her all day, had he? Hadn't he given her a dozen chances to run fast if she wanted to run fast? And instead, she'd offered him solace and restful common sense and the natural perspective of humor. She was a wonderful lion tamer. She'd certainly handled him better than he'd handled himself, which had slightly aggravated him.

He was no longer aggravated; he no longer needed solace. An expert on survival, Tanner knew exactly what he needed. This. The feel of her arms winding around his neck. The texture of her warm supple lips moving beneath his. And the liquid sheen of desire in her eyes that was just for him.

In good time he lifted his head, saw Charly's trembling mouth and took a long harsh breath. He lifted her collar and started buttoning her jacket. "We're going home."

"Yes."

"Your home. Because you have horses to take care of in the morning."

"Yes."

"It's a long drive. We'll have more than enough time to talk."

"Yes."

"If you don't stop looking at me that way, we're not going to be talking. We're not even going to make it to the truck." His scolding didn't have much effect. She just stood there looking lost and beautiful and willing. Heaving an enormously humorous sigh, he firmly tucked her against his shoulder and steered her through the parking lot.

"One of these days," he said dryly, "I have to decide whether you're dangerous for my peace of mind or whether you are my peace of mind, Charly. Although I really think you took that decision out of my hands weeks ago."

Charly heard him. Once he handed her into the ice-cold truck seat, she huddled, freezing, until he started the engine. Her nerves were shattered and her heart was shuddering. Men kissed women all the time. Tanner must have kissed hundreds of women. She was fairly sure none of them shredded into emotional confetti after a single kiss. Obviously her reaction was inappropriate. *Melting into the floorboards would also be inappropriate, Charly, so put yourself back together.*

"I need to make a quick stop at a drugstore. You need anything?"

"No." But again, she barely heard him. She knew exactly what to do with an upset, uptight, troubled Tanner: love him, Charly style. Her problem was that her heart distinctly wanted to be loved, Tanner style. She had good common sense. She was a practical, capable, responsible woman everywhere and with everyone—except near Tanner.

He didn't talk until he'd pulled onto Third Street and headed away from town. By then the heater had started pouring forth warm air, and she'd put a clamp on her emotions. "I want you to know about my job. I need you to know," he said quietly.

"I'm listening," she responded, and meant it.

His gaze flickered briefly to her face. "You didn't seem so willing to listen this afternoon."

"This afternoon you weren't looking for someone to talk to," she said calmly. "You were looking for someone to chew on."

His response was immediate. "I would never have chewed on you."

"Nonsense. You would have chewed on anything you could see. I wouldn't have minded if that would have helped. But when you start talking with a chip on your shoulder, Tanner, I generally don't hear anything that matters." In minutes the city lights were gone and the only thing ahead of them was a black ribbon or road bordered by low mountains of moonlit snow.

"What matters," he said finally, "is what I figured you could see. I have a job, but not a job that most women could live with, or would want to live with. For good reasons."

"You're telling me the reason you haven't married." Her tone was soft, careful.

"I'm telling you the reason I couldn't."

She leaned her head back and closed her eyes. "Tanner, you're scribbling fast but you haven't put the pen in the ink. I can't outguess you. For heaven's sakes, say what you want to say in plain English."

She supposed he tried, although he never really told her anything specific about his job. She understood that his work with the Customs' Service Contraband

Enforcement team had gradually evolved into government service of a completely different kind.

"What I say can't make any sense to you unless you understand that all countries have a system of regulations and laws affecting border control. In our case alone, you're talking at least a half dozen agencies that have a slice of that 'border control pie'—police, Customs, FBI, CIA, conservation, state authorities . . . even the U.S. Forest Service has jurisdiction in these northern borders. And the Canadians have a similar lineup.

"Even though everyone has the same goal—of peace—the laws inevitably overlap and good intentions get bogged down when there are that many people involved. You lose time. You lose the ability to act quickly. Sometimes a life just won't wait to be saved until a dozen agencies agree on the appropriate action. Sometimes the chance to prevent an international incident may not wait for a committee decision about jurisdiction. Both countries know this. And a long time ago, both countries decided they needed someone to act like a liaison, a troubleshooter. Are you following me?"

"Yes." But she was really listening to what he didn't say. Tanner was describing a life-style where there had never been anyone to count on but himself. He didn't talk about courage any more than he talked about loyalty and conscience and commitment, but those, she'd figured out a long time ago, were inseparable from the man he was. Finally she understood the lost look of loneliness.

"When I was sent home, I figured it was the best of both worlds. I knew the area. I was tired of roaming and I thought it would be simpler here. I figured there'd be time to build up my mother's ranch again, claim some roots...." He hesitated. "I'm two years past thirty-five and I figured I'd paid my dues. Long-term, I planned to get out."

"You've changed your mind?" Charly guessed.

She watched him pat his chest pocket like a man who'd once been a smoker. It was the only sign of nerves he showed. "I must have thought it through a hundred times. It always comes down to the same thing, whether I want it to or not. This is what I do, what I believe in. I don't know how to turn my back on it."

"Then why try?" she asked quietly.

He shot her a sharp look of impatience. "My work involves risk, Charly."

"That was more than clear."

"So that's not a problem, if I'm alone. It's insurmountable if there's someone else involved. Where I come from, a man doesn't expose anyone else to his choice of risks."

There'd been a time to let him talk, he'd obviously needed to, but there was also a time to let a man have it. "I hope you're not proud of that attitude, Tanner."

His eyes only left the road for seconds, but his dark gaze was startled.

Tanner wasn't going to buy anything soft-soaped, so she didn't try. "You read Donne in ninth grade just like everyone else. No man is an island, and you're smart enough to figure out that any man who tries to be is either bananas or a self-righteous patronizing turkey. *You* decided not to share your risks with an-

other human being? You're not God, buster. Other
people can decide for themselves what they can and
can't handle in the way of risk."

"Charly, I—" He paused. His voice changed from
hoarse to humorous. "You're not saying anything I
thought you'd say."

"What did you think I'd say?"

"*Anything* but a lecture on 'patronizing self-
righteousness.'"

While he was still thinking, she leveled a last shot.
"You chose a rough road. Maybe there's no making
that easy, but don't forget that lots of people never,
never find something that matters to them. Really
matters. I have that something in my Belgians, so did
you honestly think I wouldn't understand?"

"Understanding and being able to live with are two
different things. It's not that simple."

"Anything that matters is always simple," she corrected him. "That starts with air, water, food, shelter—and needs. The need to fill the hours in a day with
something you value. The need to have someone to
share those hours with. What else could possibly make
a difference?"

He fell into silence, but as he gave his full attention
to the road she saw his frown fade, the tension in his
shoulders ease. He started to say something once and
then stopped. While he was lost in concentration,
Charly, regrettably, mentally played back everything
she'd said to him.

It was nearly an hour before his truck dipped in her
drive and the headlights beamed on her horse barns
and paddock. An hour was ample time for the long
emotional day to take its toll on Charly.

Before he stopped the engine, she was pushing at her door handle. By the time he closed his door, she unconsciously slammed hers.

"You're mad?" he said across the whistle-harsh wind that had come in the night. He sounded disbelieving, startled.

"Of course not. What on earth would I be mad about?"

"I always expected you to be upset about my work—"

"I am not upset about your work. Why should I be?"

"Because most women would be?"

She threw up her hands. "I am not most women, Tanner."

"Believe me, sweetheart, I know that." His gaze lanced her face as sure as a spear would a target. "Was it something I said?"

"No."

"Something I did?"

"No! Would you stop this? There's nothing wrong!" But there was, and she strode toward her back door as if riled-up devils were nipping at her heels. Everything she'd said to Tanner in the truck was lashing back at her.

She didn't regret yelling at him. He'd the same as said he'd cut himself off from personal relationships for all the wrong reasons. Tanner had such a thick head; someone had to yell at him. The right woman wasn't going to be scared off because of his job. The right woman had more brains, and more heart, than to ever come between a man and his commitments.

Only Charly suddenly realized how that lecture must have sounded coming from her. Presumptuous. Embarrassingly forward. And worse—oh, lord, even worse—as if she'd been making hints she thought she was the "right woman" for him.

She pushed at the doorknob, snapped on the back-hall light and pivoted on her heel. Tanner was looming right behind her like a tall shadowy bear, the wind catching his shag of dark hair and the light the metal glint in his eyes. "I'm coming in," he warned her. "At least until I find out what you're so upset about."

"I'm not upset, not at you, and I never said you couldn't come in."

"No? You had a look in your eyes that made me think you wanted to slam the door in my face." His mouth twisted. "You still do."

"What do you think I am? Two years old? I've never slammed a door in anyone's face in my life." Still, she blocked his entry, too darn scared to let him in. Letting Tanner in had repercussions she wasn't sure she could face. Letting Tanner into her life had always had repercussions she wasn't sure she could face.

"You're going to tell me what's wrong." He said it gently, but his eyes said something about the immovability of rock.

"Nothing is wrong. Exactly." She took a quick breath, then blurted out, "You can come in, you're welcome in, as long as you're here for your own sake. I don't need any man doing me any favors, you understand?"

"*Favors?* What the Sam Hill are you talking about?"

Now he was the angry one, angry enough to stomp the rest of the way inside whether she wanted him to or not. Unlike her, he was totally conscious of slamming the door.

Pulling off her boots gave her a perfect excuse to duck her head. She really didn't want him to see her face just then. "I don't know how to say this, Tanner. But if you've been spending time with me just to be nice, I'd just as soon you headed back out the door. I know it must have looked like I pushed my company on you from the beginning, but that was because I thought you needed a friend. And so did I. I just want it clear that I wasn't pushing myself on you as a . . . as a woman. Or I never meant to give you that impression. You don't have to—"

"I don't have to kiss you or touch you or make love to you? Is that what you're trying to say?" He jerked off his boots and jacket, mad enough to spit. He had no idea what had brought on all this nonsense from Charly and didn't want to. He wanted to shake her. Hard. "And if I ever hear you put yourself down like that again, I will!"

"You will what?" She glanced up, at first confused. And then alarmed. "Now wait a minute—"

"Don't you dare look scared. You know damn well I'd shoot a leg before harming one hair on your head."

Maybe she knew it, but her pulse fluttered with panic when in one rough motion he pushed off her jacket and grabbed her. She ducked, which had the equivalent effect of an ant trying to budge the Rock of Gibraltar.

He anchored her head between his palms and took her mouth. It was a heathen kiss, uncivilized, unfair, unprincipled, a searing of lips, a taking of tongues, a man's mating stamp. She couldn't breathe. He didn't care. She couldn't think. He didn't care. He hadn't finished stealing one kiss before he was stealing another, and his deft clever fingers were already pulling at her red mohair sweater.

"You think I have to do this? At least you got that part right, Charly. Because I do. Have to. Do this."

Her hair crackled like lightning when he pulled off the sweater, and cool air shivered over her skin. His mouth had already descended on hers again when she heard the snap of her bra.

His lips lapped the path of her exposed throat. A calloused hand cupped her bared breast. In one blind second she knew he wasn't going to behave. Shame, restless and ruthless, climbed in her bloodstream. Because in the next blind second she knew she didn't want him to.

She knew him capable of great tenderness, but at the moment he was power and darkness, life and fire. From the first she'd been vulnerable to Tanner, but not like this. This was an exotic lush fall into every fantasy she'd ever had. This was a coming together like she'd die if she didn't. This was need sharper than a whip, excitement that burned. This was everything she was afraid of...laying bare how much he mattered to her...laying bare that when she was with him, she wasn't plain Charly at all but a wildly sensual woman, a sultry mate to match him, beautiful. How embarrassingly foolish that she felt so beautiful when...

"If you don't start helping with clothes soon, Charly, you're going to be the only one naked."

"You're crazy! We're in the back hall!"

"I don't care where we are." His teeth closed on the soft skin of her throat. "Neither do you." He found the beat of her pulse. Licked it. "This is what happens when we're together. I turn hot. Then you turn hot. Then the sky starts exploding and—never mind."

He grabbed her wrist and started pulling. He stopped in the middle of the dark living room, apparently because he suddenly developed a total intolerance for civilized attire. He had them both stripped and bare before she could think.

"If you think I'm going to seduce you, Charly, you're mistaken. It's going to be the other way around. You're going to take what you want, exactly what you want, and when it's done you're going to know damn well I'm not doing you any favors. You ever use a stupid word like that anywhere near me again and I swear I'll—"

He never finished the scold. He was too busy kissing her throat, and she had the heady sensation of falling. The carpet made a rough cushion for her spine even before she recognized the shift in gravity. Tanner didn't give her any time to think about gravity. His lips fastened on her breasts. He worried the nipples into taut, aching wet tips with his tongue, and then he did it again.

"Touch me, honey. Touch me like I want to be touched, like I need to be touched. You know how."

"I have no idea how," she whispered.

"Yes, you do. Make me need. Make me want. There's no one on this sweet earth who can do that as well as you can. Do it, love. Show me."

It was like asking her to tease a lion, to woo a sleeping bear out of his cage. Only Tanner was already less than manageable, less than controlled, and at the first contact of her cool palm on his throat, he sucked in a dangerously wild breath. In the dark living room, surrounded by the sweet scent of pine, she suddenly breathed in the promise of his dare. And then the reality.

He'd dared her to make him need. She couldn't. He'd dared her to make him want her. She didn't know how; she was afraid she'd look foolish and untried and inadequate.

Tanner's face suddenly loomed over hers, his eyes the devil's silver and his whisper like velvet. "There are times to play it like a lady, sweet. That isn't now. I want your legs wrapped around me. I want to be buried inside of you. I feel need like a fever now, but you could make it worse. If you wanted to, you could make it so much worse. You want me climbing walls? You want—"

She covered his mouth with her own. It stopped his slow lazy taunt and started her own. Everything he'd said was disgracefully wicked. Her entire life she'd craved—just once—to be wicked. Deliciously wicked. And his tongue was waiting for her, waiting to encourage every immoral fantasy she'd ever had.

Her pulse grew fitful, her bare body damp with excitement. They tangled and twisted on the carpet. She kissed his thigh, his wrist, his navel, his nose. Maybe those first kisses were experiments, tests of his inhibitions, his wants, his responses.

Only the feel of his sleek supple skin acted like a drug. It was like the robber who'd already held up the bank. Too late to repent now. Stealing one intimacy was hopeless momentum to steal another. She was the female pirate; he was the treasure. His taste, his textures, his scent, his coiling muscles and heat and his hair-roughened thighs wrapping around her; she wanted it all.

She was so sweet. Sweet as a man's lifeblood, nectar for a craving thirst, but Tanner was drawn even more by a vision of exactly how high he could take her. Need ripped through him. Not a pretty need, but a primal one. Watching her come alive as a woman was the bittersweet pain of having missed her, all these years. Of thinking loneliness was all there was, all these years. Of never believing there could be anyone for him, all these years.

"Are you going to take me, honey?" he murmured. "It's so easy. I'll show you how easy, and I'm prepared for you this time. The only thing you need to worry about is being so damned high you can't stand it...."

He coaxed her to climb onto him and slid his hands down to her hips, where he could help her. If his mouth molded on hers, her tongue melted his. Below, her slick slippery softness began to enfold him, and he felt a spear of fire.

He urged her to go slow. She ignored him. He'd have died before hurting her, yet her instinctive contractions nearly hurt him. She was tight. She was warm. She took all of him inside her, then withdrew; she sheathed him in a glove of warmth; she abandoned him. The only thing in his head was making it good for her, but at that precise moment he could have clawed steel.

And when he opened his eyes for one brief second, he saw her smile. It was so dark, so shadowed in that room, but her smile was pure woman, pure exultant brazen woman. To hell with sex. Charly was high on Charly.

"Since you offered for me to do the taking," she whispered, "I think I may. In fact, I think I just may experiment with driving you clear out of your head." She hesitated. "If you don't mind, Tanner."

He couldn't breathe, much less think. "I love you, woman. How the devil could I mind? Take us. As far, as hard, as fast, as wild as you want to go."

The lady did.

Shamelessly.

And later, long into the night, he woke her up simply to kiss her. Dozens of times. She undoubtedly didn't understand what she'd given him.

He did. He could damn well have everything if he had Charly.

Nine

In the pale morning light, Tanner watched her sleep. Her hair had tangled around her throat. Her lashes half fluttered open and shut—she was dreaming. When she stirred next to him, cuddling closer, the slight movement bared part of her shoulder.

He reached down to lay his lips on her sleep-warmed skin and then, because he couldn't stop himself, possessively lifted the curling tangle of hair from her neck. Once her throat was exposed, he laid his lips there, too.

She smelled sweet. She tasted sleepy. And she wakened like a ticklish kitten, all stretches and curls and lazy blinks of her soft green eyes. "What time is it?" she murmured.

"Past time for me to go. Past time for you to be up and out with your horses." Still, he kissed the shell of her ear, meltingly slow and leisurely. He eased back then so he could have a look at her face. No woman ever in this lifetime had looked at him as though he were the sun and the moon. Just her.

Her lethargic smile faded when she noticed the grave lines on his brow. Her fingers sneaked out of the covers to smooth them away. "Suddenly so serious?"

"You have a problem, honey."

"I'm aware. No wonder you weren't sleeping. Have you been suffering this condition long?"

"Not that problem." He praised her teasing with a kiss. "I'm talking about a serious problem." Warm heat flooded her cheeks when his palm stroked the side of her hip. "I warned you about my job, Charly. You didn't warn off very well."

"No?"

He swept the bangs from her forehead, kissed her temple. "A lot of people have accused me of being insensitive, cold. From the day I met you, I've been trying to warn you about that, too. You didn't listen."

"Maybe a lot of people don't know you very well."

"Maybe a lot of people aren't you. Maybe, Charly, you're everything in a woman I thought I'd never find." She was tensing. He sensed vulnerability as sure as a hunter, which wasn't the reaction he expected from her at all. Not after last night. Not after yesterday.

"You don't mean that."

"I love you," he murmured low. "I not only love you. I need you. You've given me back something of myself. Maybe it's courage. Maybe it's just believing in myself again. I don't care what it is." He pressed a fluid soft kiss on her temple. "All I know is that I'm not letting you go. And if it's all right with you, I'd just as soon skip an engagement and put a permanent emerald ring on your left hand.''

''You're talking crazy.''

''You'd rather have a diamond?''

''Tanner! I'm not arguing about rings. And if you don't stop this, I'm going to wrap you in a strait-jacket.''

She tried to jerk into a sitting position. He anchored a leg over her, making that choice impossible. When he cupped her chin in his palm, he took away her choice to avoid facing him.

Something was wrong. He searched her eyes and still didn't know what it was. He'd always assumed his work was the major handicap in his involvement with anyone. Charly had made mincemeat of that idea the evening before. She'd also given herself to him with a wildness and willingness that had, delightfully, exhausted him. Charly was his. He knew it. He'd thought she knew it. And no hurricane, no army, no paltry problem, was likely to take away the only view of the sun he'd ever had, but her green eyes were filled with determination. And utterly perplexed him.

''I'm not happy with what I have to offer you,'' he said quietly. ''I have the land, though, Charly, and I have money. You'll never want, and you can expand the breeding of your Belgians as far as you dreamed. I can't offer you security as most women value security, but there are dimensions of my job that I can change, that are about to change.''

''Let go.'' Her voice was soft. Soft steel.

He held tighter. ''You love me, Charly. Don't try to deny it.'' But he felt the razor slash to his heart because she didn't try. The raw emotion was bare in her eyes, unhidden, real, vulnerable.

"Let go," she repeated.

"I'm going to marry you."

"No, you aren't—let me up, Tanner."

He only released her when he realized there was real fear in her eyes, which astonished him. She scooted out of bed and reached for her robe. Daylight glowed only seconds on her bare breasts and abdomen before, like a curtain closing, she wrapped the robe tight. "There is nothing you have to change about your life or your job. Not for me, and certainly not for the woman you end up marrying."

She'd covered her bareness as though she thought it was a sure way to cover vulnerability. He could have told her she was badly mistaken. Charly looked as breakable as glass when she knelt on the corner of the bed and faced him. "You're not thinking," she said softly. "You met someone when you were lonesome and tired of roaming, Tanner. You met someone you could trust. At least, I hope you trust me, because believe me, you can. I can prove that trust right now, love, by promising you I'll be the best friend you'll ever have. But never your wife."

He wanted to interrupt her, yet her fragility stopped him, her obvious battle with pride. Whether or not Charly knew it, there was moisture tangling in her eyelashes and the color had drained from her face. By contrast, her voice was as bright and light as a breeze.

"Your future wife, Tanner, is going to be tall and beautiful and confident. She'll probably speak French and Spanish like you do. She'll probably have traveled all over like you have. When you walk down the street, people are going to say, 'Aren't they well matched.' You walk down the street with me and peo-

ple are going to say, 'He must have been hard up.' No!
Don't glare at me like that, because I'm not through.''

He kept quiet, but only with an effort. He could feel
the pump of adrenaline, the coil of emotion pushing
him.

''If you think I don't value who I am, you're mistaken,'' she said fiercely. ''I have enormous pride in
what I have, what I've done with my life. But that
doesn't make us suited, Tanner.'' She tried to smile. ''I
always hated the Cinderella fairy tale because I always figured she ended up divorced—''

''Stop it, Charly.''

''No. I'm just me, Tanner. You need to count on
someone being there? That answer is yes, always, ir-
revocably. But I swear to the heavens if you ever bring
up the word marriage again I'll ask you to leave. And
I'll mean it.''

Her soft-spoken ultimatum fell on a silent room.
Tanner's first reaction was to shake the living wits out
of her. His second was to wish for a brick he could aim
at his head.

Too late, he realized he'd heard it all before. And
that he'd never really listened, because he'd been so
wrapped up in his job and what he saw as his honor in
not involving her. Dimly he recalled her calling him
self-righteous and patronizing.

Seems she'd left out selfish, which was more to the
mark. He could have seen if he'd looked. She hid her
orchids and she hid her perfume and she'd been totally surprised when he told her he wanted her. He'd
assumed it stemmed from her naiveté with men. She
wasn't naive; she was simply and totally blind about
what a special woman she really was. She saw herself
as plain—not just on the outside but on the inside.

His gaze focused on her face, on the frame of hopelessly silky hair, the crushable mouth, the pale eyelashes and broad brow. He recalled thinking her plain when they first met, but that was a hundred years ago. Charly was the most alluring woman he knew. Sexy, hardheaded, unpredictable, sassy, exciting and so damned beautiful. *But you're not going to believe me if I tell you that, are you, love?*

"Tanner, I need to know that you understand. I need an answer."

Lightning quick, he reached across the bed to tug at her hands. "If you don't want to talk about marriage, Charly, we won't talk about marriage." She tumbled, easily, on the slippery comforter and rumpled sheets. He tumbled, just as easily, after her. "In fact, if you don't want to talk, we won't talk." Her eyes were anxious, but he caught the sheen of a stronger emotion. Her lips were framing protests, but he caught the fast pulse in her throat and the climb of heat in her skin. "You made real clear what you don't want. So we're going to concentrate on what you do. You can have everything your own way, love. Everything. Starting right now."

He couldn't lose her.

Not now. Not ever. She'd change her mind. He'd make her feel good about herself, as she had done for him. He'd make her feel strong, as she had done for him. He'd make her feel beautiful, as he saw her.

Problems were Tanner's milieu, challenges his lifeblood. Charly was his heart.

Then, that morning, nothing seemed insurmountable, because it was that inconceivable that he could lose her.

* * *

Strutting and posturing, the owl spread his wings to a full five feet the moment she stepped in the cage. "Quit showing off, George. I'm not in the mood."

He flapped his wings, which failed to get her attention. When she dropped breakfast in his food dish, she forgot to cover it. He swelled up his chest and glared at her as if to say, what was it going to take to intimidate the human this morning? But all she did was smile vaguely.

"Antsy to be free, aren't you? You know you're all better and we're nearly at the end of January. But as I thoroughly explained to you yesterday, George, we're still in the blizzard season. You're just going to have to wait a few more weeks." Charly refilled his water container from a pitcher. George fluttered down from his perch to the open cage door. The rope tether prevented him from escaping. "Tanner's not here. There's no point in looking. You certainly looked your fill when he was here last night, though, didn't you."

Her voice caught. She stopped talking, her gaze fixed past the wire cage to the open shadowed hayloft. There was no music up here, no lights, no moonlight. She'd been up with George when Tanner had stopped by, and she had to look like a cat's reject after working all day, but he'd gotten it in his crazy head that he wanted to dance. In the dark. To a "Blue Danube" that played only in their minds.

George picked up his toy mouse, shook it good and threw it at her, which brought Charly's head around, but all she did was rub her temples.

"You didn't see the orchid he brought me for Christmas, George, but it was hopelessly extravagant. I told you what my parents thought of him, and you know what he was like when I caught that cold. There are enough Godiva chocolates in the house to totally ruin a woman's complexion. I think I forgot to tell you about the black lace panties. No lady, George, *no* lady on this earth would have the nerve to wear them. Dammit, what am I going to do with him?''

George hopped, perch to perch, until he was on the rod just above her. Then he preened as if to remind her how gorgeous and magnificent he was.

Tanner couldn't really love her. His profile belonged on an antique Greek coin. Hers belonged on homespun folk art. When they came together, it was like tinder and a brush fire, but the newness and wildness of first passion had to fade. She'd been telling herself for a month that it had to fade. She'd been telling herself for a month that one of these days he was going to open his eyes and look at her, and then she'd be glad she hadn't been foolish, that she hadn't believed, that she hadn't succumbed to the illusion of being loved.

She was thirty-two years old. She knew exactly who she was. She had a gift for horses. She had determination and will. She was reasonably quick, certainly capable and stronger than most. But she was not attractive. As a child, her parents had ingrained in her that charm and style and looks didn't matter, and of course they didn't. From the time she was sixteen, though, she'd understood that she had none of the equipment to hold a man long-term, and never a man like Tanner. She'd faced the real truth a long time ago. The problem was him.

When she was with him, he coaxed her into being foolish.

When she was with him, she believed all kinds of wonderful, terrible, wild things.

When she was with him, she felt like an entirely different woman—desirable and beautiful and extraordinarily loved.

"But there is a huge difference from what I want to be and what I am, George. I've had thirty-two years of lessons in life. They won't just erase, they won't just go away. I don't see how I can make him happy, and I know what you think. You think I turn to butter the minute he walks in. Well, that's about to change. All I ever wanted for that man was to set him free, emotionally free to care about someone. And now, dammit, I seem to be the one who's holding him up."

She froze, hearing the sound of a car engine below. Her heart picked up the speed of a roller coaster, then plummeted. It couldn't be Tanner. He'd already told her he had work that would take him away for a couple of days.

Her face was drawn as she closed the cage door and headed down the stairs. She wanted to see him. She didn't want to see him. She wanted to face up to the imcompatible match, to doing the right thing by Tanner, to being honest with herself. Only she loved the man more than life.

And she couldn't take much more of the emotional roller coaster.

A definite mood breaker was waiting for her at the bottom of the stairs. Outside, the sky was a clotted fist of snow clouds, and the wind had started howling early. It was hardly a morning for a casual visitor, and from the far door she could see the peek of a Mercedes' headlights.

The gentleman hovering just inside the barn wore an impeccable wool coat over an equally impeccable suit, and his shoes were shined to a high gloss. She could see the glint of a solid gold watch when he made to straighten his fluff of white hair. Her lips curving in an instantly amused smile, Charly strode toward him. "You're obviously lost," she said sympathetically.

"Actually, no. Not if you're Miss Erickson?"

"I am. But let's make that Charly." When he offered a hand, she hastily pulled off her gloves. His handshake was firm and square and captured her attention. He was a little man, no taller than she was, yet there was a vital authority about him, and his light shrewd eyes assessed her with painstaking thoroughness. Her eyebrows feathered with curiosity. "What can I do for you, Mr—?"

"Evan White, and Evan would be fine. I'd heard something about your Belgians and hoped you might not mind my stopping by to ask you a question or two."

"Not at all." Her voice had a burr of gentle humor. There were lots of gentleman horse farmers. Even the richest of the breed knew better than to walk in a barn in polished shoes, and the weather made a chance "stopping by" highly unlikely. Never mind who he thought he was fooling, the man was an entirely welcome interruption. Anything that would have kept her mind off Tanner was a welcome interruption. More immediately relevant, her stranger's hands looked cold and so did his cheeks.

"I don't know what kind of questions you have, but it's cold out here. We can go up to the house—"

"Please don't bother. I don't want to get in your way. If you don't mind, I'll just follow you around for a few minutes. That way I can ask you my questions without interrupting your work."

"I'm not going to make you stand out here in the cold," she said firmly, but he wouldn't budge. Eventually he did just what he said. He followed her around while she ducked in and out of stalls feeding horses. "Were you interested in buying or breeding?"

"Definitely both."

Sure he was, she thought wryly. He flattened dead against the wall when the two-year-olds gamboled by him, headed for the east pasture. At the same time she saved him from the yearling who tried to nuzzle his ear, she generously volunteered information about breeding lines, stud prices, sale etiquette and vet fees.

He nodded at knowledgeable intervals, but when it came his turn to ask questions, well, he *tried*. He asked her why she fed the horses a molasses mix. What a breeding chute was. Why the stalls were a certain size. How old the horses were when she started to train them. And when silence lagged, he came up with a hearty "Do they have shoes?"

"Pardon me?"

He cleared his throat. "Is this the kind of horse that has to have shoes?"

And that was when she put down her curry comb and brush and firmly herded him into the supply room. By then his nose was red as a button and Charly saw no point in his continuing to suffer.

She gave him the only chair and, maternal fashion, wrapped his hands around a mug of coffee strong enough to put hair on his chest. That action alone seemed to put him in shock. She perched on the desk.

"We'll warm you up," she said gently, "then maybe you'll tell me why you're really here."

The mug was midway to his mouth. "I told you why."

She smiled. "You love horses just like I love tarantulas, Mr. White. And you're welcome to the coffee, but you're wasting your time if you thought I'd answer any questions about Tanner."

He never blinked or sputtered or showed surprise, but their eyes met over his first sip of coffee. Her guess had hit the mark. A dry little smile played at the corners of his mouth. "I read an entire book on Belgians before coming here," he told her.

"Wasted," she said sympathetically.

"You can't know I was here about Tanner."

"Of course not," she agreed, "but you're not, sir, a feed salesman. You're not hawking insurance or selling barns or spray material. Those are my standard intruders in the winter. From the look of your car, I figured you were maybe a lawyer, only I couldn't imagine why a lawyer had business with me, so the choices kept narrowing down."

She poured herself a mug. Although her actions were smooth and efficient, she was suddenly desperate for a fast dose of caffeine. Thoughts whirled through her mind. She trusted her first instinctive judgment. Evan was no enemy and he was a good man. Maybe he'd faked his interest in horses, but his light blue eyes were hard with honesty, and he'd risked frostbitten toes and a terror of horses to come here. Still, she didn't know what to make of his connection with Tanner, what Tanner would want her to do or say. Something, though, clicked in her mind from the way he was looking at her. "Correct me if I'm wrong," she murmured, "but I believe Tanner would shoot you if he knew you were here?"

Respect glinted in his eyes. "Remind me never to play poker with you, Charly."

She shook her head. "If you'd wanted to fool me, I'm sure you could have. You didn't try very hard, Mr. White, which would almost lead me to believe you wanted me to find you out. True?"

"Dead true," he agreed.

"Which is all very interesting, but I still don't understand. Who are you and why are you here?"

He changed on her suddenly. He was still a little man, still sitting square in the chair with his hands folded, still studying her. But somewhere she could hear the imaginary sound of kid gloves being removed and laid on the desk. His gaze sharpened and his alto laced with iron. "As far as who I am—for a number of years Tanner has reported to me. That was never a boss-employee relationship but more one of information sharing, where I kept the final judgment calls."

A gulp of coffee slid down her throat, hot and acid. She knew enough of Tanner's job to realize the gentleman had just laid some serious trust on the line. "So that's who you are . . . but that explains even less why you're here."

"I wanted to meet you."

"Which is self-explanatory. You're here. The question is why?"

"To find out if I approved of the woman who was tying Tanner up in knots. To find out if she was the kind of woman who'd be there if he was in trouble. To find out if she was ultimately going to help or hurt him."

"I..." Cotton wool seemed clogged in her throat. "Mr. White, I can't imagine where you got the impression... I think you may have misunderstood—"

"I haven't misunderstood anything and you can stop calling me 'sir' and 'Mr. White.' The titles make me feel stuffy, and as Tanner keeps telling me, I'm stuffy enough." Her heater effectively blasted out warm air. He started unbuttoning his coat, his eyes on her face.

"You can relax, young lady. It didn't take me long to figure out that in the right setting you could outclass a duchess. Actually, I'd already guessed that. Tanner would never be in this shape over a simple package of sugar and spice, which is what I came to discuss. The shape of our mutual friend."

Alarm leaped in her eyes. She tensed. "Is he in trouble? I swear if he's hurt and you've wasted all this time—"

"He's hurt, and he's in trouble, and you can just sit right back down again. Lord, you're a pair." Evan shook his head, but his mouth was an unsmiling line. Quiet, slow, he said, "He's got his mind on one thing and one thing only—and precisely at a time when I need him at his best. He's lost weight. He's lost confidence. There are times I have yelled at him for being bullheaded and blunt and arrogant. Not recently. You can either make or break that man's spirit, Charly, and I wish to hell you'd make the choice."

She felt stunned, as if someone had slapped her. It wasn't that she believed Evan so much as that she'd never considered the idea that she could hurt Tanner. "I know he's lost a little weight, but everything else you're saying...Evan, I don't have that kind of power over Tanner. I never did. You have to be misunderstanding—"

"He loves you like something clawing through him," Evan said pleasantly.

"He doesn't!"

His cool smooth voice cut like a knife. "Then let me put it another way. *If* you happen to love him, recognize that he needs someone strong enough to stand by him. Tough enough to handle him. And woman enough to be there when the chips go down. His chips are all going down next Sunday, Charly, and I'm asking you to make a choice. Either to be there for him or to let him go."

She was mortified to find herself so close to tears. None of this was the stranger's business. Evan was presumptuous and cruel and wrong. The words "woman enough" stung. The thick tight ache clenched around her heart, though, had nothing to do with this nasty little man and everything to do with loving Tanner. She said fiercely, "If for one minute I thought he needed someone—"

"Not someone. You. And as I said, next Sunday. Are you going to be there?"

Ten

A dozen cars were already parked around the circular drive when Tanner drove in, making him frown as he twisted his truck key. It was only one-forty-five. The Sunday meeting wasn't scheduled until two-thirty. Except for Evan, he'd anticipated being the first to arrive, not the last. He distinctly didn't want to be the last, because it meant he was out of time.

A mercilessly cold wind ripped at his coat when he climbed out of the truck. He should have moved quickly yet suddenly he couldn't move at all. His gaze narrowed on the tall, elegant glass-and-stone house just ahead. Inside, a gauntlet waited for him.

Evan had claimed he could take a leisurely year to ease the transition to the new job, but as they both knew, Evan lied. The sink or swim condition started this afternoon. The dozen people in the house ranged from a retired supreme court justice to a cabinet

member and environmental attorney. Discussion
would revolve around politics, drugs, private business interests, environmental concerns and the entire
tangle of laws affecting border control. However di-
verse the problems, the common goal was a peaceful
border—a goal Tanner had shared all his life. The
high-powered dozen, however, were not there to meet
him but to test him. He would either emerge from the
meeting as a man who could be manipulated or as a
leader. The tightrope was integrity. Both the Canadians and Americans inside would assume his bias. He
had to prove otherwise.

If he was capable of it.

He had to go in yet still couldn't force himself to
move. Beyond the house, through a thread of tall
black trees, he caught a glimpse of Rainy Lake. He
focused there blindly.

Once he went in, he knew what would be expected
of him, just as he knew the kind of leader he wanted
to be. Maybe he had eighteen years of direct experience and successes in the field, but it was still a giant
step up. He told himself that was the main reason for
the huge lag in confidence—and knew it wasn't true at
all.

He'd always jumped when someone needed him,
and always successfully. A man found a way to do
what he had to do. That premise was so ingrained in
Tanner that he'd never doubted it.

Only Charly needed him. And he seemed, badly, to
have failed her. Past sense, past rational thinking, past
honor and civilized values, she belonged to him. He
knew it as sure as he breathed. He wanted to protect
her. Keep her. Guard her. Love her.

His Great Snowy Owl wooed a mate by offering her
something she wanted and needed in an effort to coax
her closer, closer, closer, until the trust and love were
there. Some women wanted security; some women
needed protection. Tanner had figured that Charly
needed lingerie and chocolates and orchids. He'd
thought she'd wanted to let that so fragile, so romantic side out of hiding. He'd thought she needed to believe in her own allure, her own specialness, her own
brand of beauty. He'd thought he could help her grow
in directions she wanted to grow as a woman if he just
loved her with everything he had.

Only it wasn't working.

Or he wasn't man enough to make it work.

Or Charly just didn't love him.

Tanner mentally shook himself. *You head down that
pit road and there's no out. Where are all those guts,
Tanner? Where's all that do-what-a-man-has-to-do
philosophy?*

He thought dryly, *It's with Charly.* But he squared
his shoulders and climbed the steps toward the double carved doors. His jaw locked with grim determination, he forced himself into a professional mood.
The dozen people inside were going to demand, and
deserved, everything he had.

He hadn't reached the top step before Evan pulled
open the door. Agitated, he ushered Tanner in, mur-
muring, "We have a slightly delicate situation here."

"I believe that's the whole nature of business we
do," Tanner said dryly. His mood automatically
calmed in response to Evan's obvious and rare nervousness. Stepping into the pecan-paneled foyer, he
pushed off his topcoat. Evan was waiting with a
hanger. "They've all arrived?"

"Yes."

"Why so early?"

"Because we had a slight change of plans. Just wait a minute. Don't go in yet. You need to be in a proper mood before you go in there."

"Evan, I've never had a 'proper' mood in my life," Tanner murmured, still trying to fathom his boss's mood. Evan was fussing with his cuff, blocking the doorway and studying him as fiercely as a prof would a prize student. None of that was particularly unusual except that Evan wasn't meeting his eyes. Tanner tried humor. "No Stetson, no cowboy boots. The suit's banker gray and I swear I brushed my hair. Sorry, Evan, but I just don't shape up better than this."

He won no smile, just a vague "You look fine."

Then silence. Those hawk eyes finally met his. Tanner had never seen the impeccable Evan so distressed. "I'm the one who's supposed to be nervous, not you." He couldn't keep the humor from his tone. "If you're afraid I'm not up to snuff—"

"You were always up to snuff, Tanner. You're going to shine like fresh rain. It's just—"

"You forgot to fill me in on something?" Tanner guessed.

Just beyond the pecan-paneled hall, he could hear the drift of conversation, clipped Canadian accents blending with distinct American drawls. Thanks to Evan's tutoring, Tanner was prepared to connect names with faces—assuming his boss ever moved aside and let him have the chance.

Momentarily, Evan was busy handwringing. "Not about the group, exactly, but there is a little something I need to mention. The problem, Tanner, is that

I'm afraid you're going to be irritated, and this is not a day we need to test your temper—''

"If you ramble on much longer like this, I'm going to bend down and sniff your breath," Tanner warned him, but his gaze abruptly narrowed on the view just past Evan's shoulder. No one lived in the house. It hadn't been used for anything but meetings in years. However elegant the facade, Tanner had been led to expect minimal furniture and minimal amenities inside. Just beyond Evan, however, was a massive silver urn filled with an extraordinary mass of peace roses.

His gaze jerked to Evan, who suddenly couldn't talk fast enough. "No, we don't usually have roses. We usually head for a conference table and plug in a coffeepot and rough it." A peculiar expression crossed his face. "She had other ideas. Next thing I knew, she had a tea party set up. The natives certainly came in restless, but now they've been fed, watered and charmed for the better part of an hour. I'm not saying it was a bad idea, but she does have a habit of taking over, doesn't she?"

"She?"

"She took out my conference table, took away my ashtray and had me moving furniture all morning. Tanner, I am sixty-seven years old. I do not know how to arrange roses." Evan bumbled on. "I know you haven't set a date yet, but when you do—I'm attending the wedding. She already asked me. Pity she already has a father. I could have stood up for her."

Tanner was no longer listening. His head came up like a wolf scenting the wind. None too gently, he moved Evan aside and strode toward the double French doors leading to a great room. Fire lapped in a giant stone hearth; on the mantel there were more roses. Big comfortable chairs circled the fireplace. The round table between them was groaning heavy with food, cheeses and finger sandwiches and fruits and dips and . . . Oreos.

He caught a moving slash of red, but a dozen men rose when he came in and surged toward him. Greetings and handshakes were exchanged, and for several minutes he had his hands full. As Evan had warned him, the military representative from Canada was almost inaudibly soft-spoken, the supreme court justice had the caring eyes of an aging Mark Twain, the Quebecois communications man was more comfortable in French. He'd nearly forgotten all that. . . .

Their greetings were cordial and warm, a respect assumed among equals. Outside, minutes before, Tanner had felt totally unequal to this, out of his league, less than able to earn that respect. He was still well aware that he'd earned nothing as yet, but he would. Purpose and strength were pumping through him faster than a blood transfusion, and when the handshakes were all done, that slash of red strolled with beguiling confidence through the crowd.

The lady had her hair up. Mostly. Tendrils had sneaked down her nape and around her ears. The dark scarlet wool dress had dignified long sleeves and a demure high throat and lightly, shamelessly caressed her breasts and hips. Her lashes were darkened, her nose was powdered, her lips had a hint of sassy red, and when she blithely, brazenly wrapped an arm around his waist, he caught a distinct whiff of trouble. The scent was French. Light, elusive and dangerous.

There was the barest tremble in that slim hand around his waist. Beyond that, the lady was a poster for pride and poise.

"We've been enjoying your fiancée so much that we're almost sorry you got here so early, Mr. Tanner."

"I can see that." His arm squeezed her shoulder, which wasn't what he wanted to squeeze at all.

"I've taken up more than enough of your time," Charly said warmly. "I know you have a long afternoon ahead of you, gentlemen, so I just want to tell you what a pleasure it was to meet you and then I'll be on my way." She shook hands all around. The way the judge looked at her, Tanner was inclined to deck him, and then she glided toward the door.

"Come back here, Charly." He said it singsong and low, like the wolf in the Little Red Riding Hood story.

Conversation had already resumed; from the doorway she mouthed, "I'll be home."

To Evan, standing just past her, Tanner mouthed, "I'm going to kill you for involving her." And then he faced the room of men and, with the ease and confidence of authority, started the meeting.

It was two in the morning when he drove in her yard. Exhaustion should have caught up with him. It hadn't. He had enough coiled energy to jog around the equator a couple of times but more immediate interest in pursuing other occupations.

She'd left on the yard light. The sky was swirling snow. He left his shoes inside her back hall, his suit jacket inside on the table in the empty kitchen, his tie draping a chair in the unlit living room. Both socks were abandoned in the hall.

He had a hand on his shirt buttons by the time he reached her bedroom doorway. Beyond a night-light plugged in a low wall socket, the room was totally dark. This late, he'd expected her to have fallen asleep, and certainly the shadowed curves under the comforter were still. Extraordinarily still. Amazingly still.

"Fiancée, Charly?"

He looked intimidatingly huge and dark in the doorway, enough to make her breath catch and her mind wander to pirates and predators. One by one he plucked those shirt buttons. When he had the shirt off, he flung it.

"Yes. Fiancée. As in marriage, Tanner. You try and skip town and I'll find you."

God, he had to work to keep the grin off his face. He stalked toward her with his hand at his belt. "Someone in this room sounds extraordinarily sure of herself. You want to know what I did to Evan?"

"Please, no. I can't handle gore."

He pulled the belt off with a snap. "Who the hell do you think you are, lady?"

He was stark naked before the count of three and, blocking her night-light, presented an imposing silhouette of a physically powerful, primitively wild, paganly dangerous man.

She raised the comforter on his side of the bed. "I am," she informed him, "the woman who loves you. The lady who plans on keeping you in line for the next ninety years. And the lover who plans to exhaust you in bed for an equal length of time. Now, are you planning on climbing in or do I have to come out there and assault you?"

"You had the blood pressure raised on every one of those men," he growled.

There was a tremor in her voice, but she managed to say it. "Undoubtedly my spectacular beauty." Impatiently she patted the empty space next to her.

"I know that. I didn't know you knew that." He slid down beside her and immediately plucked away any chance bits of sheet or comforter inhibiting total contact with her. His mouth searched for and found hers, just as breast found chest, thigh found thigh and fingertips... found fingertips.

Her lips were trembling, or maybe his were. Her heart was beating so hard and wildly, or maybe that was his. He'd shared kisses with her before, but not like this one. This had the sweet yearning taste of being lost, now found. This had the flavor of once bleak desolation and loneliness, now richness. This had the spice of courage, the pepper of excitement, and the sugar... the sweet, sweet sugar of Charly.

"Tanner?" she whispered. "I'm not really so sure."

"You will be," he promised her. "We have a lifetime to work on that confidence of yours, Charly." He kissed her temple, the shell of her ear, the soft beating pulse of her throat. "You don't have as far to go as you think. Look at all that courage you showed today. I was so proud of you, love—"

"That wasn't courage." She pressed kisses on his temple, on the soft shell of his ear, on the bleating pulse in his throat. "That was realizing that you needed someone standing beside you. That was realizing I wanted that person, always, to be me. That was realizing it was about time I reached out for the kind of woman I always wanted to be." Her palms skimmed down his sides, hungry, slick, seeking. "Because I'm afraid I love you foolishly, beyond all rhyme and reason. I'm warning you, I intend to make a total fool out of myself, loving you.''

"Lord, I hope so,'' Tanner whispered, "because I have the exact same goal in mind.''

She said nothing. Her eyes were too full. And then Tanner reached up to kiss her soft damp lashes. Her arms tightened around him. He murmured something wicked and soft and loving; their lips met and then Charly took over.

A long time ago he'd fantasized about a bare nymph wantonly making love to him. About her taking him inside of her and riding him like an unbroken stallion, about her wanting him so much that nothing stopped her. She ruthlessly took his choices away. What could he do? It wasn't his fault. She so obviously, so beautifully, so preciously loved him.

Hours later, he murmured, "Tell me again, Charly.''

"I love you.''

"Not that, sweet. I *know* that. Tell me the other.''

She sighed with a sleepy good humor. "I am an extraordinarily beautiful woman.''

"And you'd better believe it.''

The sun blazed down on melting snow. There would undoubtedly be more snow. It was only mid-February, yet it was one of those rare mornings that the wind had the tang and promise of spring. Just outside the horse barn, the wind ruffled her hair as Charly impatiently latched her hands on her hips. "Do it, Tanner,'' she urged.

"You take off the blindfold.''

She reached over and lifted the white cloth from George's head. The owl blinked hard at the sharp white of sunlight, but he didn't move from his perch on Tanner's forearm. Tanner glanced at her.

"Hey," Charly told the owl. "This is freedom. This is what you wanted, everything you wanted."

George fluffed his feathers a little, then blinked.

"You think he's still weak?" Charly whispered worriedly.

"I think he's damn spoiled on loving. Your loving. And he isn't the only one." Tanner's smile was as intimate as the love in his eyes, but then he looked back to the Snowy. Slowly he swung his arm back, then whirled it up.

The owl took flight in a vision of magnificent ermine white. Tanner slipped an arm around his wife's shoulder and used his other hand to shield his eyes from the sun. George swooped low, wings flapping out of sync. When he landed on a bare tree branch, Charly held her breath, but he took off again. This second time he headed high, sky-high, as high as freedom.

"Bold and brave and beautiful," Charly whispered. Her palm, too, was tipped to shade the sun. "I thought you told me owls couldn't soar, Tanner."

"I thought men couldn't."

"Pardon?" She whisked her eyes to his, but Tanner wasn't talking. He was reaching for her.

*   *   *   *   *

Silhouette Desire®

1989
IS THE YEAR
OF THE MAN!

What makes a romance? A special man, of course, and Silhouette Desire celebrates that fact with *twelve* of them! From Mr. January to Mr. December, every month has a tribute to the Silhouette Desire hero—our **MAN OF THE MONTH!**

Sexy, macho, charming, irritating . . . irresistible! Nothing can stop these men from sweeping you away. Created by some of your favorite authors, each man is custom-made for pleasure—*reading* pleasure—so don't miss a single one.

Mr. January is Blake Donavan in RELUCTANT FATHER by Diana Palmer
Mr. February is Hank Branson in THE GENTLEMAN INSISTS by Joan Hohl
Mr. March is Carson Tanner in NIGHT OF THE HUNTER by Jennifer Greene
Mr. April is Slater McCall in A DANGEROUS KIND OF MAN by Naomi Horton
Mr. May is Luke Harmon in VENGEANCE IS MINE by Lucy Gordon
Mr. June is Quinn McNamara in IRRESISTIBLE by Annette Broadrick

And that's only the half of it—
so get out there and find your man!

Silhouette Desire's

MAN OF THE MONTH . . .

MOM-1

ATTRACTIVE, SPACE SAVING BOOK RACK

Display your most prized novels on this handsome and sturdy book rack. The hand-rubbed walnut finish will blend into your library decor with quiet elegance, providing a practical organizer for your favorite hard-or soft-covered books.

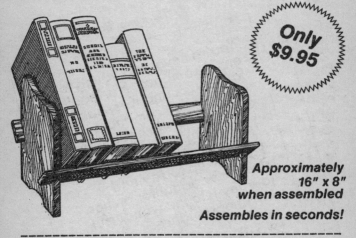

Only $9.95

Approximately 16" x 8" when assembled

Assembles in seconds!

To order, rush your name, address and zip code, along with a check or money order for $10.70* ($9.95 plus 75¢ postage and handling) payable to *Silhouette Books*.

Silhouette Books
Book Rack Offer
901 Fuhrmann Blvd.
P.O. Box 1396
Buffalo, NY 14269-1396

Offer not available in Canada.

BKR-2A

*New York and Iowa residents add appropriate sales tax.

Keepsake

◆ *Harlequin Books*